TOM SWIFT AND HIS ROCKET SHIP

THE NEW TOM SWIFT JR. ADVENTURES

BY VICTOR APPLETON II

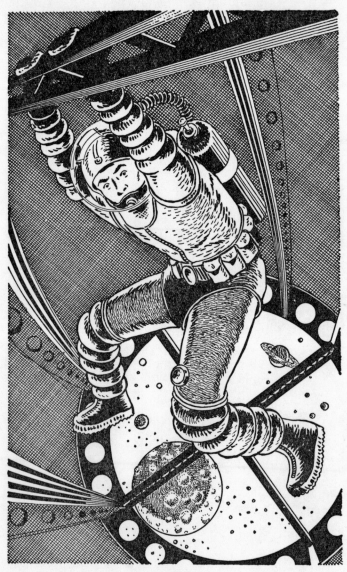

He could easily be spun off into space!

THE NEW TOM SWIFT JR. ADVENTURES

TOM SWIFT

AND HIS ROCKET SHIP

BY VICTOR APPLETON II

ILLUSTRATED BY GRAHAM KAYE

GROSSET & DUNLAP

NEW YORK

PUBLISHERS

PRINTED IN THE UNITED STATES OF AMERICA

CONTENTS

CONTENTS

ILLUSTRATIONS

TOM SWIFT AND HIS ROCKET SHIP

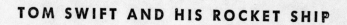

TOM SWIFT AND HIS ROCKET SHIP

CHAPTER 1

A VANISHED PILOT

"SOMEBODY'S FLYING into our restricted area!" Tom Swift cried as an alarm bell broke the midnight stillness of his rocket laboratory on Fearing Island.

The blond, eighteen-year-old scientist, tall and rangy, laid two wrenches beside the freshly machined, titanium metal column—the heart of the rocket—on which he had been working. Turning to a husky, dark-haired youth standing beside him, he said:

"Hurry, Bud! Switch on the patrolscope!"

Tense with excitement, Bud Barclay reached up to the wall and flicked a switch beneath a large screen. Three green points of light were moving clockwise in a large circle. Suddenly one of them made a beeline toward a small white dot.

"Our drone planes are after the pilot!" Bud exclaimed.

Each of the pilotless jets carried an amazing mech-

Floodlights had been switched on the instant the

anism called the landing forcer, an invention of Tom's. This instrument, directed from a beeper box in the control tower, could capture and steer intruding planes to Fearing's airstrip.

"This might be an attack to wreck our rocket base!" Bud cried.

"Let's get moving!" Tom urged, dashing toward the door.

As the boys ran from the building Tom took a quick glance at two rocket ships which stood out against the night sky. One was a pilotless dummy for a test run; the other was a needle-nosed giant in which Tom and Bud hoped to conquer space.

The wailing of the siren system shrieked over the sandy island. Immense floodlights had been switched

robots had veered toward the intruding plane

on the instant the robots had veered toward the intruding plane. The glare nearly blinded the boys as they stared upward over the center of the island.

"It's a small cabin plane—in a terrific power dive!" Tom cried.

"The interceptor drone has made contact," Bud said elatedly. "It's forcing the plane down!"

Leaping into a jeep, both boys sped past the two multistage rockets.

"Say, Tom," Bud asked, "you don't suppose that pilot was making a suicide attempt to wreck the rocket ships?"

"Possibly," Tom replied. "Certainly all licensed pilots know that this is a restricted area."

As the boys roared along the road to the airfield at the east end of the three-mile-long island, the sound of the sirens tapered to a hum.

"They're landing!" Bud cried.

Tom stopped the jeep and the two boys jumped out. Dead ahead, the fiery red glow of the robot's light outlined the captive plane as both craft banked in side by side. Tom and Bud watched tensely as the drone, only half the size of the intercepted plane, taxied in with its prize.

The instant the planes stopped, Tom and Bud hurried forward. Tom forced open the cabin door and peered in. The next moment, he drew back and cried:

"The plane's empty!"

"Empty!" Bud echoed. "Maybe it's radio-controlled."

"No, this is an ordinary commercial job," Tom replied. "Bud, I believe the pilot bailed out before the robot intercepted the plane!"

"There's a chance, then, that he's out on the water and may swim to the island!" Bud said.

"A very good chance," Tom replied grimly. "We'll search every bit of beach."

From the hangar he phoned the control tower to sound the alarm which would start an all-out search of the island and the surrounding waters.

"I'll take a copter up," Bud said, and ran toward one of the fast, new helicopters.

Speedboats roared into action from the north and south docks, and streaked away from the cone of light that covered the island. They started zigzagging, sweeping the choppy sea with their searchlights.

Meanwhile, on the south beach, Tom, carrying a walkie-talkie to keep in touch with his men, led a ground search party. It included Hank Sterling, chief engineer of the patternmaking division of Swift Enterprises, whose great skill was indispensable to the precision job of rocket building. Tom had moved most of his rocket staff from the Swift Enterprises plant on the mainland, a four-mile-square enclosure of modern laboratories and factories where he and his father carried on their experiments.

Hank scanned the sky. "The plane was coming in a southerly direction," he said, "so if my theory's correct, the pilot will be heading for this side."

"Right!" Tom agreed.

Tom Swift, the nation's youngest rocket expert,

had set up the robot defense on this Atlantic coastal island after entering the world-wide rocket building race. He hoped to be the first person to pilot a rocket into space and circle the earth in a two-hour orbital flight.

The International Rocket Society had formalized the contest by offering a one-hundred-thousand-dollar prize. When rocket research teams in several countries signified their intention to participate, the Defense Department had co-operated by declaring the thumb-shaped island to be a restricted area.

"Some of you comb the ground a few yards inshore," Tom suggested. "That pilot could be hiding behind one of the low dunes."

"You're right," Hank replied. "Some of those spots provide real foxholes."

Tom's search party fanned out and extended the hunt westward. Bud was cruising a short distance offshore, beaming a giant searchlight downward from the helicopter.

Suddenly Tom's walkie-talkie crackled and Bud's voice came excitedly from the helicopter. "I've just spotted him! He's almost at the shore. Looks all in."

Rushing to the beach, the searchers followed the beam from the helicopter and spotted the swimmer. The man was trying to combat a heavy surf and was obviously tiring fast. As the stranger's strength failed, Tom kicked off his shoes, made a long dive into the waves, and with strong strokes soon reached the helpless swimmer.

Holding the stranger's head above water, he

brought him to shore. The man, wearing only shorts and shirt, gave a great sigh, then collapsed on the sand. All efforts to revive him were unsuccessful.

"We'd better carry him to the infirmary and let Dr. Carman take charge," Tom commented.

Sterling offered to attend to him while Tom went to his room for dry clothing. After he had changed, Tom returned to the hangar to meet Bud. When the helicopter had been berthed, Tom proposed that the boys investigate the mysterious plane brought in by the robot.

"Sure thing," Bud replied. "There might even be a logbook that will tell us who this guy is. But what I can't understand is when and why he jumped."

"Because he figured that swimming in was the only chance he had of getting on the island," Tom said. "Our radar picks up boats, so he couldn't have used that method of landing."

When the boys reached the plane they found a logbook in one of the compartments in the panel board.

"Boston. Eleven p.m.," Bud read, looking over Tom's shoulder. "Edward Gates, pilot."

"Call the dispatcher there and check this, will you, Bud?" Tom said. "I'm going to alert Dad at Shopton."

Tom quickly telephoned a private number at the Swift Enterprises plant. He asked the operator to put the call through to his home. The elder inventor answered.

"What's the matter, Tom?"

"I think it's a sabotage attempt, Dad, but everything is under control." Tom explained briefly and added, "Our enemies might strike at Shopton too. Better use extra guards."

"Okay, son. Be careful."

When Tom hung up, Bud was still on the line to Boston Airport. Checking the log, he was told that the time of departure listed was precisely the same as the dispatcher's record. Bud questioned the dispatcher further about the plane's occupant.

"I'd never seen him or his friend at the field before," the dispatcher said.

"His friend?" Bud echoed. "The log lists only the pilot, Edward Gates!" He told of the single rescue. "Did he have an unlisted passenger?"

"He may have."

The dispatcher was able to give only a general description of Gates and his unknown companion, but added that Gates spoke with a slight accent and was the taller of the two. Both were dark and of medium build. Bud thanked the man, hung up, and told Tom the startling news.

"Bud! On the double!" the inventor cried. "Get the search party out again! There may be another swimmer coming in. Or he may already be on the island. Warn the guards at the rocket ships and at the lab."

"Where are *you* going?" Bud asked, as Tom started off.

"Back to the beach."

"Not by yourself," Bud cried. "Hold on, inventor boy. You're too important around here to be bumped off."

Tom paused while Bud gave instructions over the loud-speaker for a renewed search. Then, while the sirens wailed once more, the two boys jumped into the jeep and headed for the beach.

Bud, riding on the carrier behind Tom, gripped the spotlight and swung it slowly. The bright beam, shaken by the speeding jeep, moved jerkily along the dunes.

"Tom, look!" Bud cried suddenly. "I just caught a man in the spot beam. He threw himself down the minute the light struck him!"

Tom swung the wheel, and without slackening speed, hurtled the jeep toward the place where Bud was pointing. A hundred yards ahead of them, a dark-haired man, his shirt soaked and his trousers clinging to his skin, crouched in the sand.

CHAPTER 2

THE FUEL KICKER

TOM AND BUD jumped from the jeep and ran toward the half-hidden, bedraggled figure. The man held up his hands in a gesture of surrender.

"I know I'm on restricted ground," he said in a deep voice with a slight foreign accent. "But my life is more important than anything else."

The boys were a bit taken aback by this speech. If the man had made an honest error he had nothing to fear.

"Are you Ed Gates?" Tom asked sharply.

The stranger gave a start, then replied, "Why—uh—yes. How did you know?"

"From your log."

"My plane crashed on the island?" the pilot questioned as if he could not believe it.

"We brought it in," Tom replied, without explaining how. "Why were you flying in a restricted air zone?"

"Something went wrong. I couldn't bank away, so I bailed out."

Tom and Bud exchanged quick looks. Had the stranger really flown toward the island by accident? The young inventor gave the flier his sweater and helped him into the jeep.

"We'll see that you get transportation to the mainland," Tom said. "Where are you from?"

"Cincinnati. I fly business planes for the Midwest Steel Corporation."

As the jeep approached the airstrip, Gates asked, "What happened to my plane?"

"Don't worry about your plane," Tom replied. "Aren't you interested in what happened to your passenger?"

Gates' face quivered. He gulped. "Passenger?" he repeated.

"Yes. You had another person aboard, although you neglected to log his name."

The pilot hesitated for several seconds before asking, "Was he picked up?"

"Yes," Tom answered. "But he's in bad shape."

Gates bent forward and clutched his head with both hands, as if overcome with remorse. He kept muttering, "It's all my fault, it's all my fault!"

"Why did you fail to enter your friend's name in the log?" Tom asked.

"Because he wanted to keep the trip a secret from his family," Gates said quickly.

"What's your passenger's name and where's he from?" Tom asked.

"Arthur Drayton—a salesman from Chicago," the flier replied. "I've flown him several times."

"Have you your license and other credentials?"

"Right here," the pilot said, slapping his right hand against an oilskin pouch inside his soaking wet shirt.

"Good. We'll have a look at them soon," Tom said. "By the way, why did you both bail out? That wasn't necessary."

"We thought so. A plane came right at us, so we parachuted," Gates replied.

Since Gates apparently had not tried to dodge the robot, Tom's suspicions were aroused again. As they drove into the hangar, the flier appeared to be very nervous. His hand trembled as he passed over his credentials to Tom.

Everything seemed to be in order, except that there was no photograph of the man. When Tom queried him about this, he replied that he was having a new one made and had thrown the old picture away.

"I'll leave at once and take Drayton with me," Gates announced as soon as he had been given dry clothing.

Tom told him that the island's doctor was taking care of his friend Drayton, who would be moved to the mainland as soon as he was able to travel.

"But I want him to go with me," Gates said, growing belligerent. "You have no right to keep him here."

"An unconscious man doesn't have much choice," Tom retorted.

Suspicious of the whole episode and wishing to get the stranger away from the rocket project, Tom insisted that Gates depart at once.

"Drayton may come to any time now," Gates objected. "I ought to get him to a specialist on the mainland."

Tom decided the matter by telephoning the infirmary. Dr. Carman reported that the strain of combating the rough surf had taxed the patient's heart and he must not be moved under any circumstances.

"I guess that settles it, Gates," Tom said with finality. "We'll gas up your plane if you need it, and you can go—with an escort."

Gates frowned as Tom whispered to Bud. The latter dashed off, and returned in a few minutes with a stocky blond man about thirty years old.

"This is Phil Radnor of our security police," Tom said, introducing him to Gates.

Radnor nodded, looked levelly at Gates, and said, "I'll accompany you to your destination."

"You'll what?" the other man gasped, turning scarlet.

"Routine rule of this place to escort unwanted visitors off the island," Radnor said. "Come on!"

Gates looked from one to another, then shrugged. With the intruder safely in the custody of Radnor, Tom and Bud walked off. Bud went at once to the small house which was headquarters for the boys and for Tom's father whenever he came to Fearing. Chow, the Texas ex-chuck-wagon cook who spent part of his time on expeditions with the young inventor, prepared the meals.

"Well, brand my rocket roost!" the chunky, good-natured cook exclaimed, opening the door. "Say, how kin you nighthawks do with so little sleep? Now down where I come from—"

"Yes, I know," Bud stopped him. "You mean you sleep all day and all night, too," he needled.

"Nothin' o' the sort," said the indignant cook. "Say, where's Tom?"

"He went to the lab to put the kicker to bed," Bud gibed. "Has to tie his 'baby' down for the night."

The kicker was a rocket-fuel energizer. It consisted of a yard-long section of ten-inch pipe, tapering at each end into the smaller piping of the fuel lines. The bulge was loosely packed with a metallic oxide catalyst and covered at both ends with platinum gauze filters.

Tom's invention, using an alcohol–liquid-oxygen fuel combination, was designed to absorb the hyperpowerful radiation of the sun and shoot this solar energy into the liquid-oxygen supply, converting it into highly explosive, poisonous, blue liquid ozone.

With the help of the kicker, Tom's fuel would be much more efficient than any other combination yet known. In addition to the enormous combustion heat of alcohol and liquid oxygen, he would get additional thrust from the decomposition of the ozone and would decrease mass ratio.

Back at the laboratory, Tom was far from being sleepy. The excitement of the past hour had stimulated his thinking.

"This might be a good time to write up my daily record for Dad," he decided.

Tom, like all good scientists, kept a day-to-day record of his new ideas, the progress of his inventions, and his data and calculations. These records already filled several volumes. Part of it told the story of the building of his flying laboratory, *Sky Queen*, and his adventures while prospecting for radioactive ore in the Andes.

The record also logged his invention of a midget atomic submarine, the jetmarine, and the exciting times he and Bud had had in their encounter with Caribbean pirates.

Opening a small safe, Tom took out a thick, bound volume and a copy of the code both he and his father used. Since coming to Fearing Island, Tom had seen relatively little of his father. But he had kept especially detailed records about the rocket project, which Mr. Swift read whenever he visited his son.

"I feel confident now," Tom wrote in code, "that I'll be ready to launch the passenger rocket ship in ten days. I have made enough catalyst for the kicker, in spite of the rarity and the scarcity of the ingredients. Only the actual testing of the kicker remains to be done. If this test proves successful, I may have a chance to get the passenger rocket off ahead of our rivals."

Tom put the book and code away. Next, he unlocked the fuel-kicker case and carried the instrument to his workbench.

The stillness of the night reminded him that it was late and that he was all alone. Tom suddenly became aware of what an easy target he would be for an unexpected attack. He got up and looked out the window. Seeing the guard walking his post near the main door, the young inventor shook off his uneasy mood.

He hooked in the pump that was designed to carry the liquid oxygen through the kicker. Next, he attached a flowmeter to the pump to register the speed of the liquid.

In rocket flight, oxygen would have to flow through the kicker at a rate of several thousand gallons per minute to satisfy the hungry motors. Should anything interfere with this flow, the rocket would cease to operate and founder in space.

After filling the unit with red-dyed water, Tom squatted in front of the glass window in the pump model to view the flow through the kicker. He flicked on the power and listened to the even whirring of the pump.

"It's perfect!" he murmured elatedly, as he watched the scarlet liquid bubbling through the unit.

Satisfied, Tom turned off the power. As the laboratory became deathly still again, Tom was aware of a slight noise in the adjacent lab. Thinking it might be one of the chemists back to shut off an experiment, Tom, eager for company, hurried into the room.

The bright light of his laboratory revealed the intruder's face. *Gates!*

"Halt!" Tom shouted. Gates raced into the corridor with Tom after him. But before Tom lunged through the doorway, he pressed a button to sound the alarm. As it clanged, he looked up and down the corridor. There was no sign of the intruder.

"Gates must have ducked into the chemical-supplies room to hide," Tom decided. "There's no other possible place!"

Tom leaped into the dark supply room opposite his lab. Before he could snap on a light, a fist shot out and struck him. Tom lurched backward against a table with shelves. Flasks, condensers, and test tubes on it cascaded in all directions onto the concrete floor, shattering to bits.

Then everything became still. The only sound now was the drip of the acid off the shelves. A moment later Tom staggered to his feet and cautiously snapped on the light switch. No one was in the room but himself!

"Gates slipped out!" Tom groaned.

Realizing that the kicker now stood exposed as he had left it, Tom stepped quietly into the corridor. Then, treading as softly as he could, he entered his private laboratory.

Gates was bending over the kicker, trying to unscrew one of the pipes with a wrench.

Tom crept toward him noiselessly, tensing every muscle for a lunge at the intruder. Suddenly Gates straightened up and stared at the kicker. In its gleaming surface he had seen the young inventor's reflection!

Tom leaped forward. At the same instant Gates swung around and hurled the wrench. Its handle hit Tom above his left ear.

He pitched to the floor, unconscious!

CHAPTER 3

FOLLOWING A CLUE

"TOM MUST BE in trouble!" Bud thought, as he jumped from bed and pulled on trousers and moccasins. "That warning was from the lab!"

As Bud dashed outside, he could see guards and sleepy-eyed engineers running to various posts. In the distance he could hear the whine of powerboats.

Bud ran straight to Tom's private workshop. There he found his friend lying limp, and for a horrifying second Bud thought that the young inventor was not breathing.

He bent down and grasped Tom's wrist lightly in his fingers. Feeling a strong, steady pulse, he whistled softly in relief. Bud broke a vial of aromatic spirits from the first-aid cabinet in the laboratory and waved it slowly under Tom's nose. Within a few seconds the young inventor's eyelids began to flicker. Bud lifted his friend onto a couch. Then Tom groaned, opened his eyes, and sat up.

19

"The kicker!" were his first words.

To the boys' relief, the instrument stood where Tom had left it and a quick glance reassured them that Gates had not made away with any part of it. Over the loud-speaker system Tom explained what had happened, ending with:

"I guess the siren frightened Gates off. Otherwise, he would have taken the kicker."

At that instant the full import of what had taken place struck Bud. "Say, that double-crosser was supposed to take off with Radnor," he cried as the boys dashed outdoors.

"You're right," Tom said. "Before we do anything else, we'd better check on that. I have an idea Radnor got the same knockout treatment I did."

"No plane has taken off since the siren sounded," Bud told him.

As the boys stepped into the jeep, Hank Sterling hurried toward them. He said that the regular night guard at the laboratory building had been found slugged. No report had come in yet of his assailant having been captured.

Tom nodded and started the motor. He drove directly to the floodlighted airfield. Gates' plane still stood there.

Jumping from the car, Bud climbed up to the pilot's cabin. The boys' worst fears were confirmed. Radnor was slumped unconscious in his seat.

"We'd better get him to the infirmary quick!" Bud urged.

Tom lent a hand and they lifted the security officer into the jeep. The young inventor drove Radnor to the island's small hospital, where Dr. Carman took charge.

"This has been a busy night," the physician remarked, beginning his examination of his latest patient. "Hm! Radnor is in serious condition from a blow on the head. I'm afraid, Tom, that you'll have to do without his services for a while."

Tom and Bud looked at each other, telegraphing the same message to each other. Gates was not going to escape punishment for his crimes!

Before leaving the infirmary, Tom asked how Drayton was. Dr. Carman said the man's condition was only fair and that they had not tried to make him talk.

"I think we'd better fly both Drayton and Radnor by copter to a hospital on the mainland tomorrow morning," the physician stated, then added, "Tom, let me put some antiseptic on that baseball you're wearing."

After a bandage had been taped over Tom's scalp wound the boys left the infirmary, wondering where to look next for Gates. They decided first to visit the security office to see if any escape avenues might have been overlooked.

"One thing's certain," Bud said, as he looked up at the circling robot jets, "Gates won't try to fly off."

At this moment a voice boomed over the loudspeaker, "Tom Swift, please report to headquarters."

"That's the chief radio operator. Something's doing!" Bud exclaimed.

The jeep roared off to the control tower. George Dilling met the boys.

"I'm advising that you call off the search," Dilling said. "A report just came in from a boat that went out looking for him. A seaplane with an antiradar device landed and picked up a man from one of our speedboats. It took off before the searchers could get to it. I'm sure that's how Gates got away."

Bud remarked, "Gates mingled with the boat patrol to avoid being picked up. You have to hand it to the guy—he's clever!"

"And has clever friends," Tom said. "This whole deal was planned. They expected Gates to lose his plane, so they arranged for him to be picked up by the seaplane. All this must mean that he's an impostor and doesn't fly for the Cincinnati company at all."

"You mean he stole the plane?" Dilling asked.

"Yes," Tom replied. "He probably slugged the real Gates and took his credentials."

The radio operator's fists knotted with anger.

"We'll get him!" he declared. "I'll radio the mainland police, the Coast Guard, and the Air Patrol immediately. Our men are towing the boat in now."

At Bud's insistence Tom went to his quarters. But he was not allowed to tumble into bed at once. Chow, who always seemed to have the right kind of food on hand, brought piping hot hamburgers and milk to the boys' room before they were even undressed. The cook insisted upon hearing the story of the night's adventures while they ate.

"Well, brand that sneakin' varmint!" Chow exclaimed. "Things are gettin' pretty bad when livin' ain't safe even way out on a desert island in the Atlantic. Nary a critter to bother you. Nothin' but sand an' water, an' then coyotes like that hombre have to come slinkin' in here!"

Chow said good night and clumped off to his own room next to the kitchen.

The next morning, when Bud asked Tom what he was going to work on that day, the young inventor said that his first job would be to find out if the pilot who called himself Gates had been traced. Several calls to nearby seaplane bases yielded no information as to where Gates' rescue plane had landed.

But shortly before noon the Boston Airport called back to say that the plane which had landed at Fearing had been stolen, together with the rightful pilot's credentials. During the night, the real Edward Gates had shown up to claim his plane and the theft had been discovered. They had waited to call until the rightful owner could prove his identity. The identity of the strange pilot now became an even more baffling enigma.

Tom told the airport official that he would send the stolen plane to the mainland, then went to the infirmary. Upon learning that Drayton was better, he went in to see him.

"Good morning," Tom said, trying to conceal his agitation. "I understand that you're being removed to a hospital on the mainland. Before you go, would you mind telling me something more about yourself and your pilot friend?"

"There isn't much to tell," Drayton answered. "When I heard from a man in Boston that Gates was flying back to Cincinnati, I invited myself along."

"But he didn't go to Cincinnati," Tom reminded Drayton.

"No. He said he was coming here first—thought I might like to get a look at your rocket project. Then the next thing I knew he was telling me to bail out."

"And to throw your clothes and credentials in the ocean?" Tom asked.

"I didn't want to," Drayton replied, "but I couldn't swim with my clothes on."

Tom watched the man intently as he informed him that the plane was stolen and the pilot a phony. Drayton seemed shocked, but merely said:

"I know nothing about that. I'd never seen the fellow before, so if he's a fake, that's a case for the police, I suppose."

Drayton's story sounded plausible, yet Tom was suspicious. He would recommend to the police that they keep an eye on him. As the young inventor was about to leave the infirmary, Dr. Carman called him into the office. Closing the door, he said in a low voice:

"Tom, something our patient mumbled over and over again while he was unconscious might interest you. He kept repeating, 'Arthur Gray, you were a fool to get caught.' If this fellow isn't Drayton, maybe he's somebody named Arthur Gray."

"Or the guy who escaped may be Gray!" said Tom.

The more he thought about it, the more Tom became convinced this was the truth. Though the young inventor was eager to get back to his work on the rocket, he felt that the menace to the project should be cleared up first. An idea flashed into his mind and Tom went straight to the boat basin.

"Which speedboat did our visitor take last night?" he asked the attendant. "I want to examine it."

As the craft was being pointed out to him, Bud joined his friend. "What's up now, skipper?" he asked, and Tom gave him the latest news.

"See that dark mark along the bow? I believe it's paint scraped from the seaplane that landed here," Tom explained.

He bent over and began to whittle it off with a pocketknife, dropping the shavings into an envelope.

"What good is that going to do you?" his puzzled friend asked.

Tom looked up. "It's sometimes possible to trace a buyer of paint. Manufacturers have been asked to include some secret invisible chemical in small amounts in their paint so that it can be identified by police if necessary. The FBI gave me the list. Come on over to my lab, Bud, and I'll test these scrapings."

Reaching his chemical worktable, he exposed the scraps to an ultraviolet fluorophotometer.

"Look at those miniature polliwogs!" Bud exclaimed. "Is that what you mean?"

"Yes," Tom replied. He opened a desk drawer

and excitedly took out a chart. "Here it is. Worthy Paint Company!"

The boys started phoning, first to Worthy, then to a Philadelphia seaplane builder. From him they learned that the aluminum seaplane which had carried the intruder from Fearing Island was one of twenty sold to a Boston distributor only a month before.

Next, Tom telephoned the distributor and discussed the problem with him. When he had finished, the young inventor's eyes glistened. Reporting the conversation to Bud, he said:

"The dealer went through the whole list. All of the sales seemed above suspicion but one."

"What was strange about that one?" Bud asked.

"Well, the man bought three and paid cash. That was a lot of money for one man to be carrying around. Now get ready for a surprise. The man's name was Arthur Gray!"

"Good night!" Bud exclaimed. "Where was he from?"

"Hankton, Maine."

"Well, when do we start for Hankton, Tom?"

"Why not right now?" Tom replied. "We'll use the amphibian." From another desk drawer he took out several maps. "We can land in any of the coves along there. They are all open and pretty deep according to these charts."

The boys first sought out Hank Sterling to tell him of their plans. They found him discussing some wind-tunnel tests with Arvid Hanson, chief modelmaker of Swift Enterprises. Tom asked Hank to take charge of the project in their absence. A few minutes later the two boys climbed into the plane and winged out over the eastern tip of the island, circled it once, then headed northeast.

Less than an hour later Tom banked and lost altitude. Flying close to the sun-flecked waves, he hugged the shore.

"There'll be a red-striped lighthouse on the last point of land before we hit the bay we want," he told Bud.

"I see it!" the copilot cried. "Looks like a big barber's pole!"

Smoothly as a sea gull, the plane flew past the lighthouse and leveled toward the anchorage in one of the coves. A village of about ten houses hove into sight. At the end of a spit of land was a small dock.

Tom set the amphibian down about half a mile out and taxied in. As Bud made her fast to the dock, the boys saw a lobsterman, who was busy dumping his morning's catch into a square scow.

"Mighty fine plane you got there," the man observed without turning around.

"We like it," said Tom noncommittally, and asked if this was Hankton.

"That's what we call it."

"We're looking for a man named Gray," Tom said.

"The Grays is as thick around here as the pine trees," the fisherman said dryly. "You'll have to say which species you be after."

"Arthur," Tom replied calmly.

"Oh, that one!" the lobsterman said. "He ain't a local variety. But he ain't exactly jest a summer person, either. He owns a pretty fair-sized house about quarter of a mile to the right up Cove Road. Looks like a hotel. You can't miss it. But ain't no one living there now as far as I know. Not a soul."

Tom was tempted to ask about the seaplanes, but fearing he would arouse the suspicions of the fisherman, he simply thanked the man, and the two boys walked along the dock to the street.

"Boy, it does look like a hotel!" Bud exclaimed, as a huge three-story weather-beaten frame house loomed on the right side of the wooded road.

"It's closed up—just as the fisherman said," Bud remarked.

The two boys walked around the place but saw nothing unusual.

"Let's go down this path to the water," Tom suggested, "and see if there's anything there."

They walked down the pine-needled slope which led to another cove. The path ended on a pier that extended about a hundred feet into the inlet. A sheet-metal hut stood on the dock about halfway out.

"Let's see what's in that shack," Bud proposed.

The boys had just started forward when sudden footsteps sounded behind them and a gruff voice commanded:

"Don't ye move!"

CHAPTER 4

THE FIRST TEST

STARTLED by the ominous command to halt, Tom and Bud stood motionless. The strange voice growled:

"Turn around! Quick!"

The boys obeyed and pivoted to face an elderly man who carried a shotgun.

"Git goin' up that path!" he ordered, walking in a wide circle to get behind them.

"Just a minute," Tom protested. "We're not—"

"Hold your tongue, boy!" the man barked. "Mr. Gray's got me hired to keep strangers off his place. Now git goin'!"

Tom thought fast. "Haven't you heard the bad news about Arthur Gray?" he asked, looking at the caretaker over his shoulder.

"What's that ye say?" the old man asked as if he had hardly heard the question. Then, as its import

29

"Turn around! Quick!" the stranger growled

struck him, he added, "You're talkin' foolish, just to find out somethin'."

Tom said no more and started walking up the path. Bud, sensing his friend's strategy, winked at him and trudged along in silence beside him. The trio had moved only a hundred feet when the caretaker exclaimed:

"Hold on there!"

The file halted. The old man stepped in front of the boys.

"What's the matter with Mr. Gray?" he asked, peering at Tom.

"He narrowly escaped death," Tom replied. "That is, if we're talking about the same Arthur Gray. What's your boss look like?"

"Medium height, dark, has a gold-capped tooth in the front o' his mouth. He has the biggest hands I ever saw on a man his size, considerin' I never see him usin' them to do any work."

"He's the same Arthur Gray, all right," Tom said, as he and Bud tried not to show their elation at the easy identification. "He's in a hospital right now with a heart attack."

"You won't see him for a long time," Bud spoke up, hoping this bit of news might elicit even more information from the man.

"We thought by coming here we might find out about his family or friends—" Tom suggested, leaving the sentence unfinished and smiling at the caretaker.

After a moment's thought the old man set his

shotgun on the ground. Losing his look and tone of authority, he asked:

"Who be ye?"

"A couple of airmen," Tom replied. "Arthur Gray bailed out of a seaplane near an island where we were staying and we took him to the hospital. To tell you the truth, we wonder whether he's on the up and up."

"I see. Well, ye look honest enough, an' old Asa Pike ain't one to be taken in. Tell ye what. There's no place for strangers to eat around here, so come up to my house for some victuals. I might have somethin' to tell ye."

The boys thanked him and followed readily. In a few minutes they reached a shack in a pine grove. Asa Pike led them into his kitchen. A savory lobster stew was simmering on a kerosene stove.

Ten minutes later the boys were feasting on the best sea food they had ever tasted. Tom led the conversation to the topic of Arthur Gray by asking casually:

"Do many people fly seaplanes in here?"

"Mr. Gray done a lot of seaplane flyin'."

"Did he ever fly this type?" Tom asked, taking from his pocket a small photograph of the aluminum seaplane.

"That's exactly the kind!" Asa Pike exclaimed. "Land sakes! There was three o' them here about two weeks ago."

"Where are they now?" Bud queried.

"Can't rightly say," Pike replied. "They was flown

away from here by three fellers who gave me the jitters."

"Why?"

"Well, they'd been stayin' in the big house off an' on for a couple of days at a stretch while Mr. Gray was away. They only seemed to come here lookin' for mail. An' when it didn't come, they near to had a fit."

Tom asked Pike to describe the men. The first two were blond and he had never heard their names. But when he described the third man, whose name was Ed Johnson, the boys sat up and took notice. He was certainly the pilot who had stolen the plane and the flying credentials of Edward Gates.

"What kind of mail came here for these men?" Bud asked the caretaker.

"Some from New York, some from European cities," Asa replied. "Always air mail an' registered."

Tom asked the old man if he did not think it strange for such people to be in Hankton when apparently they had no interest in vacationing at the spot.

"Yes, I did," Asa Pike admitted. "But down here we figger on mindin' our own business. He pays me reg'lar for lookin' after his place, an' I can't prove he's done anythin' he shouldn't."

While Tom finished a second helping of the tasty stew, he came to a decision. He would take Asa Pike into his confidence.

"You're a loyal American," he said with a smile. "Bud here and I feel sure that Gray and Johnson and their friends are up to something underhanded, possibly to do with a big project Uncle Sam is interested in. How would you like to help find out?"

Asa Pike's eyes bulged. "Me!" he exclaimed. "Ye a-deputizin' me, ye mean?"

"Oh, you don't have to unless you want to," Tom told him quickly.

"Ketch me sayin' no," the caretaker said. "Anythin' to help Uncle Sam. Jest wait until I tell—"

"You must keep this under your hat," Tom cautioned him. "And now, can you think of anything else about the letters that might help us?" he asked.

Asa thought a moment. "The ones that wasn't addressed to Mr. Gray bore the name Marvin Hein," he recalled. "I guess that's all."

"Do you know which direction their seaplanes flew when they left here?" Tom queried, making a mental note of Hein's name.

"Northward," Asa replied.

"Better not say a word to anyone about our visit," Tom warned Asa Pike, adding, "We'll have to go now."

The boys thanked the friendly caretaker for his help, and Tom gave him their full names and the Fearing Island telephone number. He asked to be notified the minute anyone showed up at Gray's residence.

"I won't fail ye," Asa Pike promised.

The two boys headed for their plane at the fishermen's dock. The place was deserted; even the lobsterman had gone.

"We picked a good time to drop in," Bud remarked, as they cast off and prepared to taxi out to the open bay.

"As soon as I've checked the solar radiation effect on my rocket-fuel kicker," Tom said, "you and I are heading right back up this way, Bud."

The plane taxied out into open water, then Tom gunned the engines. The amphibian lunged forward and roared along the surface. A moment later it was air-borne, and by three o'clock Tom and Bud were back at Fearing Island, telling their story to Sterling and Hanson.

"Anything new here?" Tom asked when he had finished.

"I'll say," Hank Sterling replied. "The Midwest Steel pilot, Ed Gates, called up to arrange to get his plane back. He was beaten and robbed in a Boston hotel. There's no question that Johnson or Gray is the guilty one. Incidentally, our two patients were moved to a mainland hospital. Drayton never admitted to being Arthur Gray."

"I hope he's under police guard," Tom said.

"He is," Hank assured him. "Another message that came in is about your family. They're flying here in an hour." The patternmaker smiled. "Bringing Phyl Newton along—to keep Sandy company, I suppose."

Tom and Bud grinned, knowing that they were being needled. The four young people dated frequently, despite the heavy schedule of work Tom and Bud carried on.

Tom had sent for his flying laboratory, the *Sky Queen,* to be brought from the Swifts' main experimental center at Shopton. His father would fly the giant ship to Fearing Island. Sandy Swift, Tom's attractive blond sister who looked very much like him and was an expert flier, would pilot a second plane to take the visitors home again.

"I hope we get the rest of the day off, genius boy," Bud said slyly. "I haven't seen Sa—your family in nearly a month."

"No work from four P.M. until six A.M. tomorrow," the young inventor agreed.

"What's happening then?" Bud asked.

"You're piloting the *Sky Queen* as high as you can take her while I test out the fuel kicker."

At exactly four o'clock the Flying Lab roared in over the island. The flaming jet lifters lowered it onto a carpet of specially built, heat-resistant boiler-iron splash plate. A few moments later Sandy Swift made a perfect landing in a small jet plane.

"Hi, Phyl!" Tom and Bud cried, as the pretty brunette daughter of Ned Newton, Mr. Swift's close friend and business associate, opened the door and was lifted down.

"Hello, Sis!" Tom called as Sandy followed.

"Good to see you." Bud grinned. "And how did your copilot do?"

Phyl made a face. "I'll stick to riding horses," she said.

Mr. and Mrs. Swift came down the ramp of the *Sky Queen* and received a warm welcome from the boys. The older inventor and his son closely resembled each other. Mrs. Swift, who was dainty and pretty, was intensely interested in their inventions, but frankly admitted that she understood little about them.

"How is the rocket project going?" she asked.

"Very well, Mother," Tom replied. "We'll show you the one Bud and I are taking into space."

Mrs. Swift shivered a little but said she was ready for the tour. The group drove toward the launching area. Tom's mother and the girls were amazed to see how built-up the island was.

"I had no idea it was so complete," Mrs. Swift commented, as they passed the dock area with its numerous boats and the playfields for tennis, baseball, and other sports.

Then came the long barracks, the construction building, and finally the very modern-looking laboratory building.

"We'll show you the interiors after a while," Tom promised, turning the car up a road in the very center of the island. "The launching area is directly ahead."

Before the visitors loomed two gigantic rocket ships about a quarter of a mile apart. Each was painted silver gray with a red nose and at the base were three red fins on which the rockets seemed to be poised.

"The one farther over is the dummy," Tom explained, driving up to the launching area of the passenger rocket.

Set on an enormous concrete platform, it was enclosed all the way up to the nose with light-metal scaffolding. A small open elevator operated within the scaffolding.

"May we go all the way to the top?" Sandy asked excitedly.

"Don't see why not," Tom responded. "Bud, you go up with the girls. There's not room for all of us."

The three climbed up the ramp to the elevator shaft and were soon whisked to the nose.

"You're one hundred and thirty feet up," Bud announced. "Halfway to Mars before we even leave the ground."

But his audience did not smile. Instead, Sandy said, "I know Tom has taken every precaution— covering the inside and outside of this rocket with Tomasite to withstand the enormous heat from atmospheric friction. But how do you know your bodies can stand the shock of the fearful speed?"

"Our hydraulic, shock-absorbing suits will protect us. Don't worry, Sandy."

"That's all right for you to say," Phyl spoke up. "But I've read that if a rocket should leak, in the vacuum of space, a person's blood starts to boil and he—he explodes! Oh, Bud, do you and Tom have to go on this terribly dangerous venture?"

Bud smiled. "It's nice to know you'll be worried about us. But keep your chins up, girls. We'll be okay."

When Sandy said that she would like to see what the rocket motors looked like, Bud lowered the elevator car down to the launching platform underneath the ship. Both girls gulped at the maze of fuel pumps, pipes, tanks, numberless propulsion motors and platforms.

"This rocket is in four stages and each stage is complete in itself," Bud explained. "The bottom section, or first stage, directly above us drops off first, then the next and the next. Finally, Tom and I will be in our own flying stage. Now let's go back up to the pilot canopy in the nose. I want to show you Tom's latest safety device."

They huddled in the narrow elevator. Bud pressed a button and the conveyor shot to the top stage. In some ways it resembled a plane, but the girls knew that during the early part of the flight, Tom and Bud would be strapped to a board tilted at a 45-degree angle from the upright rocket. Therefore the controls had been built to be within easy reach of this position.

"See this panel?" Bud asked. "It's Tom's foolproof control. If the first three stages don't drop off by themselves, this electronic attachment will cause an explosion and off they go!"

Sandy and Phyl looked around, awe-struck. This passenger section seemed like such a tiny ship in which to make a trip through space. Commenting on this, they learned that it weighed seventeen tons, or only two percent of the rocket ship's total weight.

"But that's all we need," Bud declared. "The two bottom stages get the rocket up into space. The third is to get it in orbital motion. Our payload-stage motors are only used for braking on the return trip."

"But you don't have any windows in here!" Phyl exclaimed. "Aren't you going to be able to see anything?"

Bud smiled at her evident disappointment and said, "We do have two portholes, but it can be pretty dangerous to take a peek."

He walked over to the wall and opened a circular steel shutter, exposing a good-sized porthole in which was set an extremely thick pane of orange-colored glass.

"Tom tells me that the glass in there will absorb most of the ultraviolet light, but even so we won't dare look toward the sun.

"You see," he continued, "the blanket of air around the earth protects us from most of the harmful radiation, but out in space the sun's rays are so strong they're deadly. That's why we have these shutters for the viewing ports. But since we have another one on the other wall, we'll be able to look out most of the time from one of them. No, we won't miss a thing," Bud concluded.

"I thought it was dark as night up in space," Sandy remarked.

"True, when you're out of the planets' atmospheres. But we might pick up the lights of spaceships from Mars, for instance," Bud replied. He grinned. "So it will be easy to avoid a crash."

Sandy and Phyl were very sober. The more they saw, the less convinced the girls were that they wanted to have Tom and Bud hurtling off into space.

"Cheer up!" Bud laughed on the way to the ground. "This evening we're going to have fun and forget the rocket."

"Good," said Phyl. "When do we start?"

"As soon as we find Tom."

The young inventor, meanwhile, had been having an interesting talk with his father about communicating with a group they thought lived on Mars, who had sent a message to the Swifts. A huge, meteorlike object, obviously planned by a keen intellect, and bearing mathematical symbols had made a pin-point landing a short time ago at the Swift Enterprises plant at Shopton.

After weeks of work by the two inventors, the symbols had been interpreted as a message saying that these planet dwellers had conquered the problem of space travel. But they were unable to invent a means of penetrating the dense atmosphere of Earth and wanted the Swifts to send them a solution.

"How are you coming along on your answer to these space beings, son?" Tom's father asked.

"Slow, Dad. It's less difficult to invent a rocket ship than try to talk to mysterious people through mathematics."

"Yes," Mr. Swift replied. "I haven't had any success, either. And after we work out the message, to whom are we going to send it and how? We wouldn't want to direct a missile aimlessly into space."

Tom smiled. "It might be easier to try contacting

our unknown science friends by transmission when Bud and I are up in the rocket."

The conversation ended when Sandy and Phyl arrived with Bud, and the "evening of fun" began. Three sets of tennis, with Tom and Phyl the victors, preceded a swim. Then came dinner and dancing. Finally it was time for Sandy to pilot her parents and Phyl to Shopton.

"We'll be back to see you take off in the rocket ship," Sandy said as she waved good-by.

"Indeed we will," Phyl called.

At five o'clock the following morning Chow served the boys breakfast, and by six they were in the *Sky Queen,* ready for the test of the rocket-fuel kicker.

Tom had installed his invention on top of the great plane and also a highly sensitive thermopile to record any effect of solar radiation on the liquid oxygen. A wire led from the instrument to a thermograph in the laboratory. This would show Tom what was taking place up above.

"I guess we're ready," he said eagerly over the intercom telephone to Bud who was at the controls, with Hank Sterling beside him.

With a roar the *Sky Queen* was air-borne, climbing, climbing. The altimeter raced from left to right. At eighteen miles above the earth Tom asked Bud to hold the plane stationary.

"Why here?" the copilot asked.

"Well, the short-wave-length radiation we are looking for doesn't reach the ground. It's filtered out by the atmosphere between twelve and twenty miles above the earth. We won't get all of it here at this altitude, but enough to predict how well the kicker will work."

Tom adjusted the thermograph potentiometer to zero deflection and checked the circuit once more. Then, turning to Bud, he said, "I'm all set to throw the switch."

His voice was tense with anticipation.

CHAPTER 5

SABOTAGE

SLOWLY at first, then with ever-increasing speed, Tom manipulated the knobs that sent a flow of liquid oxygen into the kicker. The influx was at its maximum when Bud arrived to watch the experiment, leaving Hank at the controls.

Suddenly the quill on the thermograph began to vibrate. A moment later it moved up several degrees.

"It works!" Bud shouted, clapping Tom on the shoulder. "Look at her inching up!"

The young inventor stared at the thermograph, his heart thumping wildly. Part of his dream was a reality! He had solved the problem of rocket fuel! Now to install the kicker in his spaceship!

It did not matter that the quill had not advanced any farther. In a rocket the absorption of rays would be much greater. Quietly Tom said:

"We'll go down now."

Bud began to feel the awe of the situation. Without a word he turned and went back to the pilot's seat.

Hank Sterling sent his congratulations to Tom, who joined the others in a few minutes.

"No reason why we can't send the dummy rocket ship up tomorrow!" he exclaimed. "It won't take many hours to install the kicker and everything else is ready."

Upon reaching the ground, the three young men found the entire personnel of Fearing Island assembled to meet them. When the engineers and ground crew heard the good news, compliments were showered on Tom.

The young inventor grinned, thanked them, and remarked that his real work was just beginning. He would install the kicker in the dummy rocket.

"And I have another plan too," he said. "I'll rig a powerful receiver into the dummy rocket that may pick up messages sent out by space travelers on a holiday from Mars. One might even be directed on purpose toward our rocket! The transmitter will relay the message down here."

Tom's listeners seemed to be equally divided in their belief in this theory. But those who did not share the young inventor's hopes smiled tolerantly. During the good-natured argument that followed, Hank Sterling noticed, however, that the lips of one engineer, named Eskot, curled disdainfully. The head patternmaker, irritated by the man's attitude, walked over to him.

"What's the matter with Tom's idea, Eskot?" he asked.

"Why—uh—nothing. How come you asked?"

"I didn't like the look on your face, that's all," Hank said.

"My face?" Eskot spoke as if he did not understand. "Oh, you mean a look of pain? I did have a pain. Indigestion. Eggs don't agree with me. Shouldn't have eaten them this morning."

Hank Sterling walked off, not entirely satisfied with the explanation. The man would bear watching! He personally took it upon himself to trail Eskot all day, but the engineer went about his work and talked in a manner that showed nothing but intense loyalty to Tom and the whole Fearing Island project.

"Guess I was wrong," the patternmaker told himself, putting the incident out of his mind.

The next morning Tom awakened at dawn. Thoughts of the exciting launching program ahead of him kept running through his mind and he could not fall asleep again. The young inventor dressed quietly and stole out of the house.

He went at once to the giant dummy rocket ship and greeted the two guards on duty. They reported that a dozen engineers had worked all night putting the finishing touches on the project.

"What do you mean?" Tom asked quickly. "Everything was set when I went to bed."

The guards merely shrugged. They knew nothing about the intricacies of the rocket or its preparation for flight.

Tom was worried. He had left no instructions for further work. Even the elevator had been removed.

Panic seized him. Turning on the lights inside the ship, he glanced from left to right. Everything seemed to be in order in the first stage.

Quickly Tom climbed the small wall ladder to the next stage. He went on to the third, but found no evidence that any of the machinery had been tampered with.

Finally he came to the most vital part of the rocket—the fourth stage which was to return from its space flight and bring records of all kinds so that Tom would know how to proceed with his passenger rocket.

"No! Oh, *no!*" he cried involuntarily as he gazed around.

The transmitter was completely wrecked! And most of the recording machines had been put out of commission!

Tom stood dumfounded for several seconds, then he sprang into action. First, he must capture the saboteur. More than likely there was a leak in his security system. One or more of those engineers who had volunteered to work all night was the culprit.

"Working to wreck my project," Tom decided grimly. "He—or they—thought I'd never find out. The rocket would go off all right and maybe come back, but without any data!"

Carefully Tom Swift wrapped several hacked-up sections of the instruments in a handkerchief so that they could be examined for fingerprints. Finding a small hammer, which probably had been used in the fiendish act, he picked it up with a pair of pliers from his trousers pocket.

Holding on with one hand, Tom went slowly down the ladder. When he emerged, he asked the guards for the names of the engineers who had worked during the night. The men had kept no record, but between them they recalled the entire group.

"Tom! What are you doing up at this hour?" a voice behind him asked. Tom turned to see Hank Sterling coming in his direction.

"You're just the person I need," Tom said and asked his friend to accompany him to the laboratory.

Once inside the building, Tom blurted out the whole story.

"Was Eskot one of the men who worked there last night?" Hank asked.

"Yes, he was. Why did you mention him?"

Hank Sterling told of his suspicions as he helped Tom lift the fingerprints. There proved to be three sets on the hammer, but only one of these appeared on the transmitter and recording-machine samples.

Carrying the sets to the main office, Tom and Hank at once compared the fingerprints with those on file of James Eskot.

"They match!" Hank exclaimed. "I was sure they would!"

He and Tom were puzzled about the other engineers who had worked late and they decided to question each one. But Eskot would come first.

"We can nab Eskot right in his bunk," Tom said.

"I'd like to have one of our security men whisk him off the island before the others are even awake."

"We should be able to—it's only six o'clock!" Hank added.

Stepping to a telephone, Tom called Harlan Ames at the apartment connected with the control tower where the security group lived. He explained that the technician on the fuel-storage detail probably was a spy. Tom also gave the names of the other eleven who had presumably worked during the night on the dummy rocket ship.

"Hank and I will get Eskot," he said. "You and your men hold the others."

"We'll be right over," Ames promised.

Tom joined Hank who already was crossing the scrubby lawn of the crew barracks. He opened the door and they tiptoed to the big dormitory where several men lay asleep in metal beds.

"Eskot's next to the last on the right!" Tom whispered.

Suddenly a figure rose from the bed and jumped out a window.

"It's Eskot!" Hank shouted. "He must have seen us coming!"

"Look! He's running for that jeep!" Tom cried.

He and Hank also jumped out a window, but by this time Eskot was already roaring out over the clamshell road to the fuel-storage enclosure two hundred yards away.

"What's he up to?" Hank asked. "He can't escape from the island."

"No, but he can pull more foul play," Tom answered. "I believe he may be planning to blow up the tanks. We must stop him!"

"The wind's shifted," Hank cried as they raced on. "If Eskot blows up the storage tanks, the whole launching area will go."

With the speed of desperation, the two dashed toward the concrete-walled enclosure. But as they approached, Eskot brought the jeep to a screeching halt and leaped out. A second later the man was inside the enclosure. With this head start, the chase looked hopeless.

"We'd better not go in," Hank advised. "Eskot might blow us all to bits!"

Tom would not admit defeat. He was sure that Eskot had not formulated a complete plan yet. There was still time to stop his devilish aim!

"I'll go in alone, Hank," Tom called.

"I'm going with you," Hank said.

Four experimental fuels were stored in separate tanks at each corner of the huge square enclosure. As Tom looked about, trying to spot Eskot, he saw the saboteur run from the side door of a tool shed toward the ladder of the storage tank which contained fuming nitric acid.

Tom could see that the man's hands were full of highly combustible sawdust—enough, the young inventor knew, to blow the acid tank sky-high if dropped into it!

CHAPTER 6

THE ROCKET LAUNCHING

IN A LEAP Tom sprang high onto the ladder of the acid tank. Eskot was almost at the top and the young inventor worked upward at a furious rate to overtake the fanatical saboteur. He gained on him quickly.

Eskot stepped onto the metal catwalk and reached for the pressure vent through which he was intending to throw the deadly handful of sawdust.

At the same moment Tom hurled himself headlong, striking the man from behind. The sawdust scattered in the breeze.

Screaming oaths at his captor, Eskot began to fight with tigerlike ferocity. He scratched and clawed, at the same time trying to hurl Tom over the railing of the catwalk.

Hank Sterling had started up the rungs of the ladder to assist, when suddenly Eskot made a misstep while trying to avoid a lightning thrust of Tom's.

One foot groped the air and for a split second Eskot tried to regain his balance.

The effort was futile. He cracked his head on the railing and sprawled unconscious on the catwalk.

As Tom straightened up, Hank clapped a hand on his shoulder. No words were spoken, but Hank's gesture expressed his praise of Tom's exploit.

Together, they carried the unconscious engineer to the jeep and drove him to the infirmary. Tom asked Dr. Carman to keep the man a prisoner and make a note of everything Eskot said both before and after regaining his faculties. Tom arranged for a guard to stay near the traitor's bed.

As Tom and Hank left the building, the young in-

Leaping onto the ladder of the acid tank,

ventor said, "Let's find Ames and see what he and his men have learned from those other engineers."

The whole group was still in the barracks, talking excitedly. Each engineer had told the same story: Eskot had shown them an order, apparently forged, stating that the twelve were to make a final test that evening on the first three stages of the rocket.

"Presumably," said Ames, "Eskot wanted a cover-up for himself. When no one was looking, he slipped into the payload stage and wrecked the transmission and recording machines. What are you going to do, Tom?"

"Install the models that are locked in my lab." A faint smile appeared on Tom's face as he added, "It's fortunate Eskot didn't know about them."

Feverish activity was the order of the day on Fearing Island. A group of Tom's loyal co-workers, intent on making up for the damage caused by Eskot, went

Tom pursued the fanatical saboteur

over every inch of the dummy rocket ship, checking for damaged equipment elsewhere than in the nose. But they found none.

Others removed the broken instruments while still a third crew, under Tom's direction, installed a new set of recording devices. By late evening the dummy rocket ship was ready for flight.

As Tom relaxed for the first time in eighteen hours, he thought of Eskot, and immediately ordered a heavy guard to be placed around the ship. Wondering whether the treacherous engineer had regained consciousness and had confessed, Tom hurried to the infirmary.

Dr. Carman reported that the saboteur seemed to be suffering from shock more than from any physical injury.

"Even when Eskot is awake," the physician said, "he's not rational. Come and listen to him."

Tom followed the doctor to a private room where a nurse sat, pad and pencil in her hand. She reported that the patient had murmured the same words over and over again.

"He's starting now," she said, as Eskot stirred restlessly on the bed and began to mumble.

"Tell . . . Hein . . . I carried out . . . his orders! Yes . . . Johnson . . . I got it straight!"

The hoarse voice died away and Eskot lapsed once more into a deep sleep. But the names he had whispered caused Tom to grip the doctor excitedly by the arm.

"Eskot is tied up with the gang that's trying to wreck our rocket project!" he exclaimed.

"Well," said Dr. Carman, "you've collared a dangerous member."

"But there are more where he came from and there may be more on the island right now," Tom replied. "We can't relax our vigilance, doctor. Who knows what something else may happen? I think I ought to launch the dummy rocket ship at once."

"Tom, you'd better take it easy," the physician pleaded. "Get some sleep—and give your men a few hours' rest."

"I guess you're right."

That night the tall, silent rockets were so well protected by the contingent of guards that no enemy could possibly have gotten near them. As dawn broke, the island was awake again.

Fuel trucks piped the last gallons of liquid oxygen and alcohol into the dummy rocket ship. Mechanics and engineers bustled about, disconnecting fuel lines.

Tom Swift was in the nose section, with Bud Barclay watching the young inventor give his flight plan a last-minute inspection. This was an automatic pilot in the form of an unwinding, perforated tape which ran through an electric brain. Metal pins would drop into the punched-out holes and make contact with various controls.

"So you expect this piece of plastic to act as guide during the trip and bring the last stage of this rocket right back to the island?" Bud asked dubiously.

"I sure do," Tom replied. "And when it lands, not even the robot jets will have to guide the rocket in."

There was a buzz on the intercom. Tom switched on the receiver.

"Everything is clear," came Arvid Hanson's voice. "Any further instructions?"

"None. I'll be right down."

The young inventor made a final check. Then he glanced at his watch and set the tape in action. It would run blank for exactly fifteen minutes.

"Flip on the transmitter, Bud," Tom ordered, as he himself started a dozen recording machines in motion.

Then quickly the two boys descended the ladder and stepped outside. The rocket ship was sealed.

"We'll go right to the tracking room," Tom said.

They hurried to the high covered platform and watched the sensitive recording equipment which would follow the rocket in its flight. Here stood also the computer that was to receive messages from two oscilloscopes in the rocket's nose.

Every man who was not needed at another post had come to watch the launching. Among them was Chow in his very loudest red-and-green plaid shirt. He edged close to his boss and at once began to ask questions.

"Tom, when will that there kicker cut in?" he began.

"It's set to go into action at an altitude of forty-one miles," Tom replied.

"Forty-one!" Chow exclaimed. "Brand my nightmares, why do you wait so long?"

"Well, below forty-one miles there just isn't enough sunshine, Chow."

The cook heaved a great sigh. "Well, you should

have gone down to Texas then. There ain't no place where there's more sunshine than Texas," he said.

Hank Sterling moved to the public-address-system microphone and looked at his watch which had been synchronized with Tom's.

"All personnel leave the launching area at once!" his voice boomed. *"X minus two minutes!"*

Two mechanics ran for cover. The area was deserted. In the control office, Harlan Ames flicked the interceptor switch to neutralize the drones.

"X minus one minute!" Hank Sterling announced.

Every crewman on the tracking level crouched at his post as the seconds ticked toward zero. Electric movie cameras at several points were grinding the dramatic take-off footage. The men who were to operate the radar plotting equipment nervously tested the points of the pen recorders.

Tom stood as rigid as a statue. In one minute he would know whether the tape recorder would set the machinery in motion to send the rocket on its space journey.

"X minus twenty seconds!" Hank's voice was tense.

Tom gripped the railing of the platform, his eyes fixed on the poised rocket.

"X minus one!"

A multicolored cloud of gases burst from the take-off motors and the giant rocket ship lifted itself clear of the ground. The fiery explosions shook the island.

"She's away!" Bud cried.

A cheer went up from the onlookers as the rocket ship moved slowly at first, then zoomed upward. It became a pin point and finally disappeared into the sky.

Tom glanced from dial to dial. All was going well. A sudden jagged mark appeared on the white paper strip.

"The base stage has been jettisoned with its parachute!" he cried. "Now for the kicker!"

The young inventor kept his eyes glued to the dial. For several seconds there was no activity. Finally the needle flickered, crept forward, and became still. Then it trembled steadily for ten seconds.

"The kicker's getting it now!" Tom cried. "Getting plenty of solar radiation!"

The needle showed a regular pulsation.

"Bud!" Tom cried. "Come here! Watch this while I write down the figures. Note the number of degrees the temperature rises above the black line!"

"Does the line indicate the temperature without the kicker?" Bud asked.

"Yes," Tom grunted. "See what it's doing now!"

Bud peered at the dials. "It's streaking past the old mark!" he cried. "Now it's stopped rising!"

"What's the reading?" Tom asked excitedly.

"I can't believe we've hit 4900 degrees beyond the old mark!" Bud announced.

"This is fabulous!" Tom exclaimed. "We'll have power enough to take us anywhere in the universe!"

"When do we push off?" Hank asked.

"Next Friday," replied Tom.

"Next Friday!" Bud retorted. "I thought you needed another ten days."

"I did, too," Tom said. "Until I saw this."

"Boy, I can't wait!" Bud burst out. "Imagine, Tom, we'll be the first ones to do what kids have been imagining all these years!" He chuckled. "You're going to put 'Gyro George and his Space Raiders' right out of business!"

Hank Sterling and Arvid Hanson came to the platform and Tom asked them to record the testing figures while he stepped over to the oscillograph.

"Oh, man!" he cried.

"What's up?" Bud asked.

"There's a triangle coming up!" Tom responded, as he watched one impulse after another appear to form the symbol.

This was followed by a still larger triangle surrounding the smaller one, then several other mathematical forms. Tom jotted them down.

"Say, genius, I asked you a question," Bud prodded him.

"It's true! They're after us again!" Tom exclaimed.

"Who? Johnson's gang?" Bud asked apprehensively.

"No. The space beings," Tom said with great excitement. "The same ones who carved the symbols on what we first thought was the meteor. This is a follow-up message, asking our help to get them to Earth."

"Did the message come direct—or by way of the rocket?" Hanson asked.

"I don't know," the young inventor admitted, "but I think from the rocket."

"Second stage has been jettisoned!" Bud called.

At the same moment a new set of symbols began to appear on the oscillograph. As Tom copied them, he tried to figure their meaning. From his long study in translating the first group, these symbols were easily deciphered.

"What now?" Bud called.

Tom grinned. "Those Martians—or whatever they are—have sent a message of congratulation!"

"Honestly?"

"That's the way I interpret it."

Bud gave a shout. "Boy, you're the first person on this earth to get a message like that! Hey! There goes the third stage!"

It was exactly twelve minutes since the second stage had broken off. Now the tracker showed that the rocket was going into free flight.

"She ought to start back now!" Tom said, holding his breath.

"She has! She has!" Bud exclaimed a minute later.

The indicators showed that the nose section was arcing back toward the earth. Would the rocket carry through on the flight plan? Or would it crash somewhere, perhaps in a thickly populated area?

CHAPTER 7

A CRACK-UP

AS THE TIME approached for the rocket to become visible, all eyes on Fearing Island scanned the
sky.

"We should see stage four within five minutes,"
Tom muttered, his fingers clenched tightly in the
palms of his hands.

He glanced at his watch again—it was seven
thirty. He heard a commotion in the crowd and then
a shout. He looked up again and there it was—a pin
point in the sky.

"It's coming!" Bud almost screamed the words.

Straight toward them the rocket hurtled, spitting
long tongues of blue flame. Involuntarily, everyone
prepared to run. Then, as if by magic, its speed decreased. Hundreds of feet above the watchers, Tom's
invention actually slowed to a snail's pace and glided
in to a stop not ten yards from where it had taken off.

Now, only one third its original length, the rocket stood there as mute evidence of Tom's success. The young inventor ran to it and gazed fondly at the stubby red-and-silver ship that had traveled so speedily to where no man yet had been. For a short while Tom hardly heard the acclaim he was receiving, but finally he became aware of the shouts of praise, and acknowledged them with a pleased grin.

"As soon as this baby cools off," he said, "we'll inspect the recordings."

An hour later Tom broke the seal and with Bud hurried inside. First he inspected the kicker.

"It's in perfect shape, Bud!" Tom exclaimed.

One by one, the boys read the various charts. Each report boosted their fondest hopes.

"I guess you and I have nothing to worry about now in regard to our trip in the passenger rocket," Tom said at last. Then he sobered. "Unless someone else gets ahead of us in the race."

"Or unless Eskot's friends manage to stop us," Bud added.

Tom reflected on this for a second and said thoughtfully, "Bud, I think you've really made a point there. Sabotage couldn't beat us for good, but it certainly could slow us down enough to put us out of the race. Just to be on the safe side, I think I'll call Dad to make some spare rocket sections while he still has the equipment and jigs set up."

Tom had hardly spoken when a guard came to tell him that there was a long-distance telephone call for him. Thinking the caller must be his father, wanting news of the rocket-ship flight, Tom was amazed to hear a strange voice say "Hello."

"Yes?" Tom replied.

"This is Asa Pike up in Hankton, Maine."

"Oh!" Tom said. "How are you?"

"Listen!" the caretaker of the Gray estate said. "I'm callin' to tell ye to git up here as soon as ye can. Marvin Hein an' Johnson, that pilot what escaped from your rocket base, will be here this afternoon."

"What time, Asa?"

"Two o'clock."

"We'll see you!" Tom replied. "Thanks for letting me know, and keep this quiet."

"You betcha."

Tom hurried back to Bud and told him they were taking off at once to see what Hein and Johnson were up to in Maine.

"I'll warm up an amphib," Bud offered, as his friend went to tell Sterling and Ames of their plans.

"Take it easy," Ames advised. "If there's any sign of trouble, call the FBI. Don't you get in the middle of it."

"Okay, Harlan. But before I report these men, I want to be sure that they're the fellows we're after."

Bud had the amphibian ready when Tom came running across the sand to the dock. Tom hopped into the pilot's seat and they were soon winging north from Fearing Island.

"Who do you think is the big boss of the gang— Hein, or Gray, or Johnson?" Bud asked.

"None of them. Probably someone we've never

heard of," Tom replied. "And my hunch is that he's in the employ of a nation which isn't entered in the rocket race."

"But why?"

"We know about the Australian group and the English team, and that a new rocket society in Sweden is building a ship. While we don't exactly know what their plans are, we're sure that they are not trying to steal somebody else's know-how. This gang we're up against probably hasn't been able to solve the fuel problem, so they're out to steal a formula."

"Suppose they succeeded, Tom," Bud remarked, "and did get a rocket into free flight. They'd be able to establish a space platform out in the two-hour orbit and rule the world from it."

"You're right, Bud," Tom said soberly. "And what's more, I believe that's exactly their objective!"

Thinking about this terrifying problem the two fliers remained silent. But just after the amphibian had flown past Boston Harbor, Tom pointed out a mountainous fog bank lying ahead.

"That's bad news!" Bud cried. "Guess we'll have to climb over it."

"I'll call the Weather Bureau and ask about the fog," Tom replied.

The bureau reported that the treacherous "soup" had closed in over the whole coast line from Nova Scotia down and extended several miles inland. It would not burn off for hours.

Tom switched off the radio and took the plane above the dense vapor. When they reached the area where he planned to come down, Tom began to lose altitude. The fog was so thick that the boys could not see more than two feet ahead. Tom set the automatic pilot.

"By dead reckoning we're almost there," he observed presently. "I have a hunch we're just a bit to the east of our cove and about ten miles out in the bay."

"Think you'll be able to set her down in this stuff?" Bud asked.

"It's too risky on instruments," Tom said, worried. "But look, Bud!"

Up ahead a rift in the fog showed the water below. Tom instantly banked through the hole. A moment later the hull bit into the cold, sullen Atlantic.

"You did it, Tom!"

The two boys breathed sighs of relief as the amphibian churned through the water. They had gone only a hundred feet, however, when there was a fearful ripping sound outside the plane.

Both boys were hurled to the floor of the cabin, and the amphibian was jerked about as if it had been hooked by a giant grapple. It flopped over on one side, and the cabin began to fill with sea water. Tom cut the engine and reached up to open the door.

"Come on, Bud!" he cried. "We'll have to get out of here quick!"

His friend nodded, braced himself, and boosted Tom through the open hatch.

The plane was settling fast.

"Give me your hand!" Tom yelled.

He reached down and grabbed the wrist of the heavier boy who was already in water up to his chest.

"Our amphib's sinking!" Bud groaned. "Now what are we going to do?"

The fuselage disappeared a moment later and with a hissing sound the craft rushed under the swirling surface.

There had been no time to get out the life preservers. The boys tore off their jackets and shoes, and floated on their backs for a moment to get their bearings.

"Whatever happened?" Bud exclaimed.

"We ran against something—no idea what," Tom gasped.

"Listen!" Bud commanded.

A powerful boat engine was throbbing nearby.

"Ahoy there!" Tom called.

Not until the boat had come almost within reach of the boys were the men in it able to see them. They were fishermen who had heard the plane but were unaware of the crack-up.

"You sure came at just the right time," Bud remarked as he and Tom were hauled aboard.

The jovial weather-beaten captain told them that they had run afoul of the heavy fishing nets.

"That's why we were snapped forward so hard," Tom observed.

"Sorry about your plane," the skipper said, "but I'm glad you fellows are okay. The nets are covered by insurance, so don't worry about them."

After thanking the veteran fisherman for the rescue, Tom said, "All I'm worried about right now is where we are and how we're going to reach the place we started out for."

"Almost into the Bay of Fundy!" the captain replied.

"Far from Hankton?"

"Forty land miles," the skipper told him.

Tom groaned. He looked at Bud and exhaled heavily.

"I guess that takes care of our meeting," Bud said.

"You're supposed to be in Hankton at a certain time?" the captain asked.

"Before two o'clock," Tom explained.

"It's only 10:45 now," the captain said, looking at his watch, "and we sure aren't going to do any fishing without nets. This is really a speedboat converted into a fishing trawler. But she's fast. We'll get you to Hankton in about two hours and a half."

"Great!" Tom cried. "Can you do it in this fog?"

"Know the way by heart." The captain laughed. "Men," he said to his crew, "how about fixin' these fellows up with coats and shoes? And help 'em dry their other things."

The boys were quickly taken care of, then went to stand near the captain who was piloting. The speedboat was soon knifing the water at twenty knots. As noon approached, the sun created a bright glow through the thick haze.

"It's breaking some," the skipper observed.

"A little fog will be better for carrying out our plans," Tom murmured to Bud.

"Assuming it didn't ground Hein and Johnson somewhere else," his friend rejoined.

"If this fog lifts a bit more," the captain remarked, "we can hold our speed all the way in!"

It did lift considerably for the last three miles. As the craft streaked in wide open, the fishing dock and the two adjacent coves of Hankton loomed up ahead.

"Bud!" Tom whispered. "Two aluminum seaplanes are here!"

"I see the one at the main dock," Bud said in a low voice. "Where's the other?"

"At Gray's dock," Tom replied. "The point of land is hiding it now."

"Where do you want to land?" the skipper asked.

"The main dock—dead ahead," Tom replied. He decided that it would be the least suspicious place to come ashore.

The boat made a neat approach and touched without a tremor on the opposite side of the dock from the suspect seaplane.

"That was a fast run," Tom said. "We're here ahead of schedule. We sure appreciate your help."

"We owe you two coats and two pairs of shoes," Bud said. "We'll send 'em up by Christmas!"

The boys waved good-by to their rescuers, then started cautiously along the dock toward town. The place seemed to be deserted.

Suddenly they saw Asa Pike appear from a side street. He stumbled toward the boys.

"Something's happened to him!" Bud cried.

CHAPTER 8

STOWAWAYS

AS THE BOYS raced up to Asa Pike, he limped toward a pile of lobster pots. Motioning for silence, he beckoned them to follow him around the pile into a weather-beaten shed.

When they had crowded into the small shack, the old man related that Hein and Johnson had entered Gray's house while he was trying to telephone Tom a second time.

"You see, they came in early, on account o' the fog, I guess, an' I wanted to warn ye," Asa went on. "So I started to call ye. All of a sudden Hein comes an' grabs the phone out o' my hand."

"Then what happened?" Bud asked.

"They locked me in the root cellar an' went upstairs," Asa continued. "I finally managed to break out through a weak board. The outside doors were locked, so I had to sneak in the house an' jump out of a window. I near busted my leg."

"Too bad," said Tom sympathetically. "Better not use it for a while. Are Hein and Johnson still at the house?" he asked quickly.

"Yup. Heard their voices after I jumped."

"Good. Bud and I will go right up there and investigate," Tom said. "But you'd better wait in the general store, Asa. It'll be safer for you, in case of any trouble. Can you make it alone?"

"I kin git to the store all right," Asa said. "But ye fellers better do some fast thinkin'. I'm sure from what those two men said that they'll be flyin' away pretty quick. They got their mail."

He explained that Johnson's plane was the one at the public dock. Hein had brought in the other.

"Come on, Bud!" Tom urged. "Asa, if we don't see you again on this trip, let us know anything else you find out."

"You betcha."

With Tom in the lead they ran toward the public dock where one of the aluminum seaplanes was moored. As Bud sprinted along, he called:

"What are we going to do?"

"Stow away!" Tom replied. "We'll hide in the luggage compartment."

"And fly with Johnson, maybe to the gang's base?" Bud asked.

"Exactly! As soon as we've spotted their hide-out, we'll try to take over and head back home with our prisoner!"

"Then go back and capture the rest, you old bloodhound?" Bud grinned.

Tom nodded as he climbed down the wooden ladder to the seaplane's pontoon and entered the cabin. Bud followed. A few moments later Johnson came walking rapidly down the dock. Tom and Bud slid feet first into the luggage compartment behind the pilot's seat, closed the door, and stretched out on the floor.

"Wow! We just made it!" Bud said.

Johnson's clattering strides stopped. Squeaking sounds indicated that he was descending the ladder. Tom and Bud felt the plane shudder slightly as Johnson stepped onto the pontoon. They waited tensely, hoping that he would not open the compartment door.

Johnson immediately started the engines. The seaplane taxied away from the dock and skimmed across the water. In a few minutes it was air-borne.

The pilot flicked on the radio which crackled noisily. He tuned it a bit finer, then called Hein.

"Everything okay here, Marv. How about you?"

"Same here." The answer was followed by a low chuckle. "Lucky we got away before that guy Swift showed up. He must have wised up Asa Pike, somehow."

"Well, we're rid of 'em all now," Hein remarked. "No need to pick up any more mail. And now that we have some sort of an idea of how Swift's fuel kicker works, it won't take Rotzog long to figure out how to build one."

Inside the luggage compartment Bud gripped his friend's arm. So these spies, working together, had stolen the secret! And their probable leader was someone named Rotzog!

The radio was switched off and the boys lay in darkness listening to the dull roar of the motors. Tom wriggled over on his side to see a tiny pencil of light entering their otherwise dark prison. A faulty rivet had apparently become dislodged.

He managed to work his way over to the wall, and by placing his face right against the metal plates, he could look out through the rivet hole to see an endless stretch of tall timber and a sprinkling of tiny lakes. A brilliant sun shimmered on the water's surface. Tom guessed that they had ridden about a hundred miles inland.

"We must be in the Canadian woods!" he whispered, feeling sure that he recognized the terrain.

For another half-hour the plane flew at high altitude and then it speedily began to descend.

"Be ready to do what I tell you, Bud!" Tom whispered. "I'm going to take Johnson by surprise!"

"Okay!" Bud said softly.

During the long ride, Tom had been formulating a plan. He removed his belt and asked Bud for his.

Suddenly the radio silence was broken. They heard Hein say:

"Ed, I'll go in first."

"I'll be right on your tail," Johnson replied.

The plane went into a sweeping bank.

"I must work fast!" Tom told Bud. "When I yell your name, take over the controls!"

"Right."

As quietly as possible Tom opened the compartment door. With a catlike movement he hurled himself at Johnson, looping one of the belts down over the arms of the startled pilot. At the same instant he switched off the radio. His move was just in time to prevent Johnson's outcry from being heard by Hein.

"Bud!" Tom yelled, jerking Johnson sideways from the seat.

As the man fell to the floor, Bud slipped into Johnson's place and put on the automatic pilot. Then he turned to help Tom.

Johnson, who had been caught unawares, was quickly bound and gagged. Tom forced him into the luggage compartment, then called:

"Bud, turn on the radio again. We don't want Hein to become suspicious. I noticed their special wave band is marked 14X."

Tom crawled back. Bud had leveled the plane, and now at a thousand feet the boys could clearly discern the entire shore line of a large lake, deep in the wilderness.

Since the radio was on, neither boy spoke a word but Tom pointed. Scattered in several small clearings along the water front were buildings and tanks of various heights. On the top of one tank were painted the words:

EXCELSIOR OIL CO.
EXPERIMENTAL STATION

Bud turned the plane sharply to the right in order to give the boys a better glimpse of the place. But the plane had already overshot the clearings and the trees blocked their view.

"What's the matter?" Hein called suddenly on the radio. "Are you in trouble?"

The boys stared at each other. How to answer? Hein, who had already landed on the big lake, radioed his question again.

"Okay," Tom replied, trying to imitate Johnson's voice. "Just taking a look at something."

Hein called back and suggested that Johnson waste no time coming in. Tom and Bud grinned. It had worked! Now for another look at the clearings, then streak off with their captive!

Tom took over, but a moment later a new movement on the lake arrested his eye. A delta-wing sea jet came from under cover and taxied across the water.

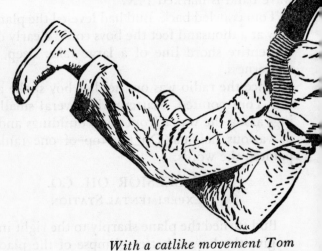

With a catlike movement Tom

"We'd better get out of here fast!" Bud yelled before he realized that the radio was on. He groaned in dismay. He had ruined Tom's plan!

Instantly Hein began giving instructions to the jet pilots to intercept the seaplane. Tom nosed the plane over into a steep dive as he saw the jet climbing almost vertically to intercept him. He opened the throttle wide, decreased the dive angle, and roared toward the far end of the huge lake.

"I'll go back along the treetops," Tom decided.

hurled himself at Johnson

Over the radio Hein's voice commanded, "Land here immediately or you'll be strafed!"

Disregarding the warning, Tom stayed in the power dive and thundered toward the water. The jet flipped over and tried to catch the seaplane's underbelly with short bursts of gunfire. The bullets sprayed the cabin, some of them burning small holes into the aluminum wings.

"They really mean business!" Bud groaned.

Approaching the water, Tom pulled out of the dive, cut the power, and leveled off toward the trees. The jet, drawn far out of position by the passes it had made, now came sweeping in again to make another run.

Suddenly the port engine sputtered. Then it coughed and died.

"Get ready for a crash!" Tom cried. "I'll brake her all I can!" With that, he lowered the flaps.

Looking ahead, he saw the timbered shore line looming at the end of the narrow cove they had just entered. The jet, losing its target behind the high pine trees, peeled off and disappeared.

But the seaplane, still traveling too fast to land on the water, skimmed along the length of the cove and plowed crazily into the rocky shore!

CHAPTER 9

AN INVENTIVE ESCAPE

TOSSED ABOUT violently in the cabin, both boys were stunned by the crash. Tom was the first to recover and crawled to where Bud lay, still dazed.

"Bud!" he cried, gently slapping his friend's cheek. "Come on, boy! We've got to get out of here. They'll be back to strafe us!"

Bud shook his head slowly in response.

"Okay, chief," he said, sitting up and managing a weak grin. "Lucky we're still in one piece!"

Quickly the boys got to their feet and looked at their captive. Johnson, too, apparently was only stunned.

"As long as he's not hurt, let's drag Johnson into the woods and leave him," Tom said. "We'll come back later and get him."

This accomplished, Tom plunged ahead.

"Where are you aiming?" Bud asked.

"I think," Tom replied, "that the only way out of this trap is to get to that clearing ahead. I spotted it just before we crashed."

"Suits me," Bud said, and after looking around at the wilderness, added, "Lead the way, trail blazer!"

For the next hour the boys, ignoring their injuries, continued toward the clearing Tom had spotted. Finally Bud saw a path. They followed it and moments later emerged on a corduroy road.

"Well," Bud remarked, "the going won't be so tough now."

Their relief was short-lived, however. They heard the whir of an approaching helicopter and dived for cover. A bullet ripped into the floor of the forest only ten feet away!

When another shot struck directly in front of them on the road, Tom and Bud looked around frantically for a safe hiding place. Seeing a tumble-down shack a short distance from the road, they raced toward it.

Unfortunately, the shack proved to be a decoy. Suddenly a stranger with a rifle clutched in his hands came silently toward them from the shadows.

The man shot into the air. Then, pointing with his free hand, he motioned the boys to walk out to the road again. With no other choice they glumly obeyed. To their relief, the shooting had stopped. Evidently their captor had fired to announce that he had caught the intruders.

The helicopter lowered to treetop height and a heavy rope ladder was dropped. A short, dark man in a white flying suit appeared on the ladder below the hatch. With a wave of his hand he gestured for Tom and Bud to climb up.

"We'll make a bargain," Tom called. "You let us go and we'll tell where one of your men is a prisoner!"

Silence!

"These fellows aren't very talkative," Bud complained. "Ouch!" he cried as their captor's rifle jabbed into his back.

Tom wondered why they were not interested in Johnson. "They must have picked him up!" he decided.

Still no word was spoken by the fliers as the boys climbed up to the cabin, where they saw two other men. The ladder was hauled up, and the craft, rising high above the trees, started back toward the clearings on the lake.

As they neared a wide peninsula that jutted into the lake, Tom saw a sprawling complex group of camouflaged fuel tanks and buildings that resembled his own experimental rocket project. It was almost as big as Tom's on Fearing Island. This was no oil company's experimental station!

Before Tom could nudge Bud to look at the place, blindfolds were tied about their heads. The helicopter was lowered and the boys were escorted out. They were marched in silence a few hundred yards. A door squeaked and they were abruptly yanked to a halt.

Their blindfolds were removed, permitting the prisoners to see that they were in a large room. Their guard, without a word, turned on his heel, slammed the door and slid a bolt on the outside. They heard him stride away.

"These guys must be foreigners!" Bud whispered to Tom. "They probably didn't want to give away their nationality by talking!"

Tom nodded. "That's my opinion. And, if the gang has a test base this size," he said, "I suspect that they must have a super rocket like our own somewhere."

"Who are they then?" Bud asked. "And where's their main base?"

"Two man-sized questions!" Tom replied. "I wish I could answer them."

He surveyed their prison. It was a sparsely furnished, one-room building of strong wooden construction. Two windows, one in front and one in back, high in the walls, were barred.

"Boost me up to this front window, Bud, and I'll take a look outside," Tom said.

His friend swung him upward with an easy movement.

"We're at the edge of the woods," Tom reported in a whisper. "There's a big cargo seaplane at the dock being unloaded. Oh—oh, a bearded character's heading this way!"

"Let me see him!" Bud said softly, and they exchanged places.

The man, holding a rifle, stationed himself at the door of the shack.

Tom, meanwhile, quietly inspected the window.

The frame and the bars were made of aluminum.

"If I only had some mercury and a glass of water, we could get out of here!" he said, getting down.

"Sure," said Bud. "If I had a bomb, I could blow us out."

Tom smiled and continued his examination of the room. Suddenly he stopped.

"Just the thing!" he whispered excitedly. "That thermometer on the wall. Bud, ask the guard for a drink of water."

"But I don't see the connection," Bud said, giving his friend a puzzled look.

"I want to try a little experiment," Tom replied as he took down the thermometer.

Bud knocked and the guard opened the door. When it became evident that he did not understand English, Bud went through the motions of drinking. The man obliged with a bottle of water, and then barred the door again.

Tom climbed onto Bud's shoulders again, but this time at the rear window. The young inventor broke the thermometer tube and let the mercury drip against various sections of the aluminum frame. Bud watched in fascinated silence. "This mercury ought to cut through the oxide surface on the aluminum," Tom explained. "Now for the water."

Bud handed up the bottle and slowly Tom poured the water on to the place where the mercury drops had fallen. The aluminum began to dissolve. After several applications, the chemical had eaten through the frame.

"Pst!" he signaled. "I've done it!"

"Honestly? Now what?" Bud asked.

"As soon as I pull these bars out, we're going to get away in that cargo plane!"

"How about the guard?" Bud asked as Tom easily pulled out the bars.

"We'll take care of him. Come on!"

Bud followed Tom through the window and dropped to the ground.

"I'll duck behind that big bush," Tom whispered. "You make a scraping sound to attract the guard. When he comes around here to investigate, jump him. I'll open the door and we'll lock him in."

When Tom was well hidden about ten feet from the building, Bud broke off a branch and swished it around on the ground. The guard heard the sound and came on a run. Soon he rounded the corner, muttering to himself.

Bud leaped on him and clapped a hand over the man's mouth. Before the guard could recover from the surprise attack, Tom had flung open the door and was back to help Bud. He tied one handkerchief firmly over the guard's mouth and with another bound the man's wrists together behind his back. The boys placed him on the cabin's cot and bolted the door.

"Now let's get out of here!" Tom urged.

Both he and Bud knew it would take only a little while for the guard to tear the handkerchiefs off. But the boys hoped that by then they would be safely away. Running at top speed through the woods, the two did not pause until they came to a small rise about a hundred yards from the cargo plane.

"We can watch for our chance from here!" Tom whispered, and crawled forward to the edge of the underbrush.

There was a bustle of great activity at the docked sky freighter. The four-man crew, jabbering in a foreign language which the boys did not understand, carried box after box down the ramp to small trucks. Finally, the pilot waved to the truck drivers.

"They've finished discharging the cargo," Tom murmured. "Now if all of them will only leave!"

To the boys' relief, the pilot and his crew hopped onto one of the trucks and rode across the clearing toward what appeared to be a mess hall.

"This is it!" Tom cried. "Dig for the plane!"

"Okay, skipper."

They raced across the rough ground onto the dock. Only a short distance remained to be covered when Bud spotted a guard atop the hangar.

"Step on it!" he cried.

Tom scrambled into the big plane. Looking back only long enough to see Bud inside and hauling up the ramp, which also served as door, he continued straight through the empty cargo space into the pilot's compartment. Leaping into the seat, he fired the starter and pushed the throttle forward. The jet engines thundered into action. Without losing a second, Tom gunned the plane out across the water and it rose into the air.

As he headed the plane southward, Tom looked

down and saw a jet seaplane taking off. He opened up all three engines and the plane sped along on its course.

"Before that interceptor can catch up to us, we'll be back in civilization," Tom thought hopefully.

A sudden cry from the cargo space snapped the young pilot out of his musing.

"Tom! Tom!" he heard Bud calling faintly.

Putting the plane on automatic pilot, Tom started back to see what was wrong. When he reached the rear of the cargo space, he stared in horror. Bud's arm was trapped in the loading door.

A strong wind could tear the door off and blow his friend out!

Tom started forward to extricate Bud's arm when a blast of gunfire ripped into the starboard wing.

"Don't let 'em get us!" Bud pleaded.

"But your arm—" Tom said.

"I'll—hold on—"

Torn between anxiety for his friend and the immediate urgency to escape, Tom paused for a split second. But another burst of fire sent him racing back to the pilot's seat, where he took over the controls. The pursuing jet was riding the freighter's tail!

Instantly Tom cut the motors and threw the plane into a yaw. The sudden braking effect which this maneuver produced forced the attacking jet to come up alongside the larger ship. In this position the enemy's guns could not be brought to bear on Tom. Tom banked sharply toward the fighter plane until his right wing tip was directly underneath the left wing of the other plane. Then suddenly he flipped up the right wing of the heavy cargo plane, to tip the tiny jet over on its side, and send it downward into a crazy spin.

By the time the enemy pilot regained control, Tom had the throttle wide open and was streaking out of range. Then he put the ship on automatic pilot, turned on the radio, and hurried back to Bud.

He was stunned to see Bud's head hanging downward, his knees sagging toward the deck. The boy was in agonizing pain!

CHAPTER 10

A ROBOT AT WORK

AS BUD fought bravely to retain consciousness—his eyes were closed and he was panting—Tom realized that his copilot might suffer a permanent arm injury.

From a block and tackle overhead he cut off a length of quarter-inch rope and tied his friend to a stanchion, so that when the door was released, Bud would not be sucked out.

Tom pressed the lever which controlled the door, but discovered that it was not working. Bud must have tried to pull the door shut by hand the last few inches, and his arm had become caught.

Perspiration stood out on Tom's brow. He had to act fast! Tying himself also to the stanchion, Tom pushed with all his might against the door. It did not budge.

He released the air pressure and then switched the control lever to the open position. As a fresh surge of compressed air hit the piston, Tom smashed into the door with his shoulder. There was a sudden explosion of air and the door gave way.

He pulled Bud's arm in and locked the door as the copilot sank to the floor. Then he rushed back to the pilot's seat and took a quick look at the terrain.

Banking downward toward the river, he could see that he was approaching the city of Montreal. Tom radioed for medical assistance, then made a neat landing on the river. An ambulance was waiting to take Bud off the moment the air freighter stopped.

"Easy!" Tom called to the medicos, and explained what had happened to his friend, who now had lapsed into semiconsciousness.

They removed Bud at once to a hospital, Tom riding along in the ambulance. While he waited for news of his friend's condition, the young inventor telephoned the police and gave them the story. They impounded the freighter, and assured Tom that they would investigate the Excelsior Oil Company plant at once and let Tom know the result.

Next, Tom put in a call to Fearing Island. He spoke to Harlan Ames and reported the latest developments.

"Lucky you and Bud got out of that place alive," he commented. "Suppose I send a plane up to bring you back."

"Do that."

Ames held the wire so that he might hear the report on Bud. A nurse came to tell Tom that his friend had regained consciousness and could be released from the hospital in a couple of hours. His arm had not been badly injured, thanks to Tom's quick thinking. Tom relayed the good news to Ames, then hung up.

An hour later, while seated in a lounge waiting for Bud, Tom was amazed to see the boy walk in, a doctor behind him. Bud's right arm was in a sling.

"Golly, it's good to see you!" Tom exclaimed. "I thought we weren't going to be able to take that rocket trip after all."

"I'm going on that trip if I have to be carried into the rocket!" Bud rejoined, laughing. "Only let's make sure the doors are shut next time."

But Tom noticed a grimace of pain cross his friend's face as his sore arm brushed against the wall.

"You're lucky not to have lost it," the doctor said. "See your own physician when you get home."

"We weren't going home," Tom spoke up, "but if—"

"What's the matter with Doc Carman on the island?" Bud said. "Let's go!"

The boys were driven to the airport where they saw one of their fast jets just coming in. Arvid Hanson was piloting it. As soon as he learned that Bud's arm would be all right in a few days, Hanson remarked wryly:

"I believe you fellows would be as safe up in space as you are on this planet."

Tom laughed. "Maybe safer."

He and Bud climbed aboard and headed for Fearing Island. When they landed a few hours later, Harlan Ames hurried over to meet them.

"You're both all right?" he asked quickly.

"Sure," Bud replied. "Meet the magic-carpet boys. The minute Tom and I are captured, we fly away."

The others grinned, then walked over to the hangar.

"Any word from the Canadian police yet?" Tom asked.

"No word yet," Ames replied.

"Any other news?"

"Yes. Your father phoned that the interplanetary gyro was ready to be picked up. Hank Sterling went to get it."

"Good," Tom said. "Bud," he added, as his friend yawned loudly, "you'd better get some shut-eye."

"How about you? A tough day for you too."

"Oh, I'll come along," Tom promised. "I want to look over a few things before I turn in."

"Okay, night owl." Bud winked at Hanson. "Watch out for a new invention by morning. But be sure to call me if Tom decides to take off in the rocket. I think he's trying to shake me off."

He was driven away in a jeep by Hanson, while Tom went to the communications office to be on hand for news from Canada. Weariness finally overcame him and he lay down on a cot in one of the rooms. But at daybreak Dilling awakened him.

"We have a report you'll never believe!" he began. "The Canadian police arrived at the rocket base within an hour after they got your call."

"And captured the whole gang," Tom broke in.

"Captured nobody. The place is a ghost town!"

"What!" Tom burst out incredulously. "But how about their fuel tanks and other equipment?"

"Most of their gear was blown up or just abandoned," Dilling replied. "And the personnel had vanished—every single one of them!"

"Have you any idea where they went?" Tom asked. "Did they leave any clues?"

"No clues, but most likely they flew over the North Pole in long-range super jets," Dilling answered. "A lumberman reported seeing a large number of planes heading northeast. The police figure Hein's crowd knew that if they fled in any other direction they'd have been tracked easily."

"Sounds reasonable," Tom said. "What's next?"

Dilling reported that a guard had been set up at the abandoned base and a study of the layout would be made.

Tom's disappointment was deep. The criminals had escaped again!

In a sober mood he lay down once more and for an hour turned the problem over in his mind. He dozed off finally, but was awakened by a buzzing sound in the next room. A signal! Jumping up, he rushed out.

"Maybe it's news of those rocket men," he thought excitedly.

But the summons was for a completely different reason.

"Sterling is calling," Hanson said. "He's in trouble. A strange jet is trying to force him down! They're in a dogfight right now!"

"Did you get his position?" Tom cried.

"Yes—only two hundred miles west of here!"

"I'll go to help him!" Tom announced. "And I'll need the fastest thing on the island. That's the *Sky Queen*. Anyway, I want to tow in Hank's attacker."

Without explaining further, Tom flipped on the loud-speaker and began to bark orders to the crew of the Flying Lab to warm up the mammoth ship. Then he requested that they roll one of the interceptor robots into the *Sky Queen*. Finally he called Hanson to accompany him.

"Be ready in a minute!" Hanson replied. "Roger!"

The two met at the airfield and immediately climbed into the *Sky Queen*. As the needle-nosed drone was being fitted into the hangar of the Flying Lab, Tom gave Hanson instructions on what he was to do with the robot. Then Hanson took up a position at the remote-control unit near the small plane. This beeper had been made stationary in the hangar.

Tom had already rushed up to the second deck to prepare for the take-off. Only ten minutes had elapsed since the call for help had come!

The *Sky Queen* lunged upward in a fiery blast, and seconds later was streaking along through the sky on her way to intercept Sterling's attacker. Tom contacted Hank and learned that the fight was still on. A few minutes later, traveling at a twelve-hundred-mile-an-hour rate of speed, the Flying Lab arrived on the scene.

Far below, two small black dots were maneuvering

wildly. The *Sky Queen* bore down toward them.

"Okay, Arvid!" Tom called on the intercom. "Go to work on him! Come up behind with the robot!"

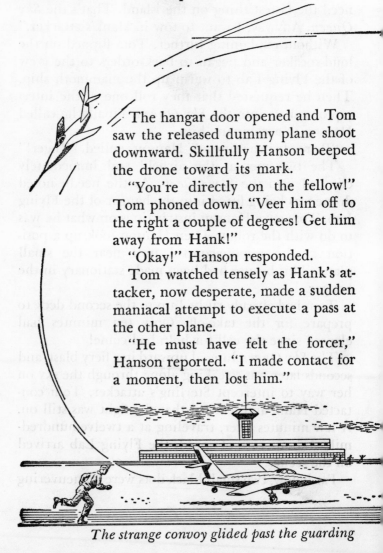

The hangar door opened and Tom saw the released dummy plane shoot downward. Skillfully Hanson beeped the drone toward its mark.

"You're directly on the fellow!" Tom phoned down. "Veer him off to the right a couple of degrees! Get him away from Hank!"

"Okay!" Hanson responded.

Tom watched tensely as Hank's attacker, now desperate, made a sudden maniacal attempt to execute a pass at the other plane.

"He must have felt the forcer," Hanson reported. "I made contact for a moment, then lost him."

The strange convoy glided past the guarding

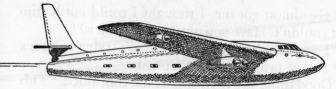

"Try again," Tom urged.

The enemy pilot was trying to come in from the right side. As he completed his turn for the new approach angle, the powerful landing forcer caught the plane in its electronic grip and rolled it violently away. Hank's jet streaked ahead, unmolested.

"We've got him now!" Hanson cried excitedly into the phone. "Are you going to ground him here, Tom?"

"No. We'll force him in at Fearing Island."

As the strange quartet of aircraft headed for the ocean rocket base, Hank Sterling radioed Tom.

"Thanks, Tom!" he said. "That robot sure is a honey. Why, it picked that plane off its course like an ace rifleman after a bird."

Tom was delighted himself with the performance of the pilotless jet robot. "Did you have a rough time with that fellow?" he asked.

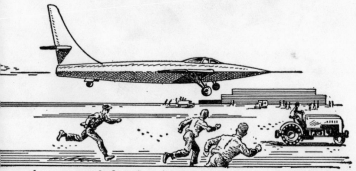

robots toward the airstrip

"He almost got me. I thought I could outfly him but couldn't. Have you any idea who he is?"

"I suspect it's part of a gang that's trying to wreck the rocket project," Tom replied.

"Good thing you arrived!" Hank continued. "This secret unit might never have gotten to your base."

"Is it okay?"

"Yes!"

"Well, you go ahead with it and land first," Tom advised, as they approached the Atlantic Ocean.

"Maybe we'll learn something from this fellow that we failed to get from Hein and the others," Tom mused, as they flew across the stretch of water to Fearing Island and circled for a landing.

The strange convoy glided past the guarding robots toward the airstrip. Hank Sterling had already taxied to the hangar.

Tom cut in the *Queen*'s landing jets and hovered to allow the two small craft to go in first. After they had reached the field, Tom lowered the Flying Lab.

As he approached the airstrip, the young inventor's pulse quickened. What clue to the enemy's identity would this latest captive reveal?

CHAPTER 11

A CODED THREAT

AS THE THREE planes landed, mechanics rushed onto the Fearing Island airfield and surrounded them. One group taxied the robot jet to a hangar, but the other men stood by awaiting orders.

Tom cut the jet lifters a notch and the *Sky Queen* settled onto the take-off disk.

As he dashed down the steps past the first deck, where Hanson was coming from the hangar, Tom called:

"Great job! You handled the beeper like a veteran!"

Hanson grinned. Together, they ran over to the captured plane where Ames joined them. The pilot sat in stony silence. He was black-mustached and thin, about forty years of age.

"What's your name?" Tom demanded, pushing back the plastic cowling.

The answer was a glare of hate.

"I'll look for identification," Ames spoke up, and as soon as the pilot had climbed out of the plane he went through the man's pockets. But the security officer found nothing.

"There may be something in his plane," Tom suggested. "Take our visitor to the hangar office."

While Arvid Hanson and several others accompanied the prisoner, Tom and Ames climbed into the jet to make a thorough search. Ten minutes later they were about to admit defeat on every count except fingerprints—and Ames felt these probably were not listed with the FBI—when Tom cried:

"Wait! Just a minute!"

He had noticed that the jet's fuselage was built of an aluminum sheathing over a laminated plywood shell. Upon investigation, Tom found that the combined thicknesses added up to only an eighth of an inch. Near the floor of the cockpit a black line of trimming ran along the wall.

As Tom inched his fingers over the area his nails suddenly caught on the trim. Over it was a thin strip of tape which he quickly tore off.

"Here's something!" he exclaimed, as his right forefinger touched the edge of a flat parchment packet tucked in between the inside wood and the metal hull. Tom snatched it out.

The pouch held three items: two air charts with routes marked in red ink and a hastily scribbled note. It seemed to be written in code, but the last word fairly jumped off the page at Tom. It was *Rotzog*.

Elated by his find and sensing its top-secret nature,

Tom thrust the pouch into his inner pocket. He and Ames hurried to the young inventor's office where Tom spread out the three papers on a desk. Starting with the charts, they noted that one traced a route from Fearing Island to the abandoned rocket base in Canada.

"This links our visitor with the spies all right!" Ames exclaimed.

Tom picked up the other map and whistled.

"Ames!" he cried. "Dilling guessed right about where those planes probably went. This course runs on the great circle from the rocket base all the way to the Bering Sea!"

The agent's eyes followed the red line that tracked north of Quebec, across Hudson Bay and Great Bear Lake, past the Yukon and far out over the Bering Sea. It ended at an infinitesimally small island, charted but nameless, in the Aleutian chain.

"That might be their main rocket base!" Tom cried. "Now we're getting somewhere! I'm going up there to take a look!"

Ames laid a hand on Tom's shoulder. "If you'll accept some friendly advice," he said, "you'll stay right here and get your own rocket into space. Let the police handle those fellows."

"You're right," said Tom, "and we don't have any time to waste, but Bud and I both have personal scores to settle with that bunch."

"Remember this," said Ames. "The rocket project of these rivals may be on the level even if it's secret. The crimes of the group that have been bothering you may be instigated by the national backers and not known to the scientists who are building the rocket."

"That's good logic," Tom conceded as he turned his attention to the coded note.

Using a code book he took from the drawer, Tom, with the security man's help, pored over the note signed by Rotzog, trying to decipher its message.

"It must be in a foreign language," Tom finally decided. "We'll have to get the FBI to help us."

The young scientist walked to the videophone, flicked on the New York circuit, and got Rick Dalton, his Northeast telecaster. Holding the paper up before the camera, Tom asked him to photograph the message from his screen and go at once to the FBI office to have it decoded.

"Call back as soon as you can," Tom urged. "I'll hold our prisoner here until we hear from you."

"Okay, Tom!" Dalton replied, and faded off the screen.

In the meantime, Tom had the equipment from Shopton moved to his laboratory. If he felt after a thorough test that the new interplanetary gyro was better than the one which had been installed in the rocket, he would make the switch.

Bud arrived, and for two hours the boys busied themselves with delicate adjustments of the intricate equipment. Before Tom had a chance to run a final check, he was summoned to the videophone.

"I have the code translation for you and wait until you hear the message!" Dalton cried.

He flashed a typed version of the note on the screen. It read:

INTERCEPT ALL TRIPS OF SWIFT ROCKET MEN. AVOID ISLAND. MEET AT CARP ON FOURTEENTH FOR FURTHER ORDERS. ROTZOG.

"The FBI is already working on the case," Dalton reported. "Anything else you want done?"

"No," Tom replied. "And thanks for the quick work."

"Who is this Rotzog?" Bud asked after the videophone was shut off. "Maybe he's the same one who was sending the letters to Hein and Johnson. Well, at least it's fairly certain that we've got the label of the top man!"

"The label, yes. But how about the location?" Tom mused. "I wonder if Carp is one of the islands in the Aleutian chain." He looked in an atlas but failed to find it. "Probably the secret name for their base," he decided.

Tom went on to say that there might be an international angle to the problem. Perhaps a foreign group had helped themselves to an island owned by the United States. He now went to interview the prisoner. The man with the thin mustache was amazed to hear what had been learned since his capture. Nevertheless, he refused to admit a thing.

"I'll have the FBI come for you and your plane," Tom told him, then returned to his work.

Bud was uneasy. Finally he admitted that he was

worried. When the stranger did not report to his superior, Rotzog probably would assign others to intercept all trips from the island and redouble his efforts to wreck any rocket launchings.

"Can't you invent an 'anti' something or other for safety?" he asked Tom. "Oh, I know we've grabbed the intruders each time so far, but I'm jittery."

Tom smiled. "I'll think up something," he promised. "What you need, Bud, is action. How about a little trip in the *Sky Queen?*"

Bud's eyes glowed in anticipation. "Where? Carp?"

"No, straight up. We still have to test my combination cosmic-ray altimeter and stellar sextant in the air."

This sensational invention of Tom's, with which the rocket pilot could know at all times his interstellar navigational position, ranked second only to the kicker.

"I thought you wouldn't need it," Bud remarked. "You have that super-duper flight tape recorder."

"Yes, but if something should go wrong with that, it would be mighty handy to know exactly where we are."

"I'll say," Bud replied. "If I get lost in space and never can fly back to this earth, it might help to know what stars I'm kicking around with."

Tom gave his copilot a friendly jab and they started for their quarters to eat lunch. To their surprise, Chow was not at the cottage and no preparations had been made for the noonday meal.

"Where do you suppose he is?" Tom asked. "It's not like our Texan to be absent."

Suddenly Bud grinned. "I think I know. Come on!"

He led the way toward a cove in the island's coast line. "I'll bet Chow's talking to his electric eels."

Tom laughed. While on a trip to South America the Texan had caught two of the strange eels which shock their prey into insensibility. Chow had decided that hereafter he would use them to do his fishing for him. Accordingly, he had brought the electric eels to Fearing Island and constructed a weir for them in the cove.

The fence was strong and had held well, but up to the moment no large fish had entered it to be shocked. Chow, still hopeful, visited his project at every low tide, no matter what time of day or night it occurred.

They saw the chef about fifty yards off shore in water up to his middle. He looked very unhappy as he waded toward the shore.

"What happened?" Bud cried. "Fish bite you?"

"Shucks, no!" Chow called back. "Ain't no fish here!"

"No fish!"

"Even lost my eels!" Chow added mournfully.

"Where's your boat?" Tom asked, knowing that the Texan always went out in a rowboat.

"Lost my oars an' I fell out o' the dang-busted boat tryin' to capture my eels. Then the boat got caught in a current an' off she went!"

Chow trudged onto the beach. Quarts of sea water oozed and trickled from his clothing and shoes. The boys howled with laughter.

"Well, brand my sea lights!" Chow said. "I thought you fellows would be sorry not to have a fish dinner." Reaching the house, he heaved a great sigh. "I'm afraid my menu for today is ruined," he lamented.

After the disappointed cook had changed into dry clothing, he prepared pork chops and a corn pudding, and topped the meal off with an apple pie he had made earlier.

Though the boys praised his skill, Chow was glum. He asked if Tom was going to South America soon and if he would bring him some more electric eels.

"Afraid not," Tom replied. "But if you want anything from a hundred thousand feet off the earth, I might oblige you. Bud and I are taking off right away for a little experiment."

"With those folks from another planet?" Chow asked eagerly. "You mean you got that lil ole gadget figured out so's you kin talk to 'em?"

Tom told him that the "gadget" was to be radio impulses in the form of mathematical symbols. They would convey a message to the space beings.

"A message about what?" Chow asked.

"It's clear," Tom replied, "that the only reason these people haven't visited us is because they don't know how to penetrate our atmosphere without being crushed to death."

"What's the matter with 'em?" Chow asked.

"I think they may have very light bodies," Tom said, "and be highly paramagnetic."

"What's that?" the cook demanded. "See here, Tom, you ought to talk English to me."

Both boys laughed, then Tom explained, "The space beings may be affected by magnetic lines of force. In that case they would be paralyzed if caught in the earth's magnetic field."

"Then they sure better stay off o' this lil ole magnetic planet," Chow declared. "We kin git along without 'em anyhow." But suddenly the Texan grinned. "However, if you see any o' these queer folks, give 'em my regards."

Chow turned and went into the kitchen. As the boys left the cottage, Tom said:

"I hope it won't be long before I can deliver Chow's message. You know, Bud, it burns me up that Dad and I can't figure out an answer to those space people. To think that they can communicate with us and we can't formulate a reply!"

"If you and your dad could concentrate on the problem long enough—" Bud got no further, for Tom suddenly snapped his fingers.

"I know how to solve part of the puzzle," he said excitedly.

CHAPTER 12

DANGEROUS ACID

FAMILIAR with Tom's sudden inspirations, Bud waited a full minute before interrupting his friend's thoughts. Then he asked Tom how he intended to solve the mysterious space beings' problem of penetrating the earth's atmosphere.

"I'll send them an explanation of how to build a degaussing shield to protect their bodies."

"Good idea," Bud said. "But how could you ever do that with geometric figures?"

"It'll be a lot of work, but I'll do it some day," Tom declared. Then, talking more to himself than to Bud, he said, "I might use an arc to represent the shield—"

At this moment the loud-speaker system boomed out the message that Tom Swift was wanted at the communications office.

"Bud, you warm up the Flying Lab, will you, while I go see what's wanted," he requested.

"Righto," Bud replied, and drove off in a jeep.

When Tom reached the radio room, Dilling and Ames were there reading a message.

"You must have news," Tom remarked.

"We sure have," Ames replied. "That first spy you caught—Drayton who turned out to be Gray—made a full confession to the FBI."

"He squealed on Rotzog?" Tom cried unbelievingly.

"That's right," the security officer answered. "Dilling just took the message. Rotzog's a crazy scientist, kind of a man without a country. Has a pile of money. Nobody knows where it comes from and it's always in cash. He pays his men well."

"To spy and steal inventions?" Tom asked.

"That and much more. Gray declares Rotzog claims he's going to rule the world from a space platform he's building."

Tom asked if the FBI had caught Rotzog, and was disappointed to learn that Gray insisted he did not know where Rotzog was, nor the location of his rocket ship. Gray had received all his orders from Hein and had never seen Rotzog.

"Gray and Johnson," said Ames, "began working for the outfit only recently and did not know much about the spy work it carried on. But one thing Gray was definite about. And, Tom, you can take a bow. Rotzog isn't afraid of any rocket builder in this world except you."

Tom smiled and said, "I'll reserve decision on it being a compliment until I find out more about Rotzog."

"Well, then, here's bad news," Dilling said.

"Rotzog has declared he'll stop at nothing to keep your manned rocket from getting into space!"

"So that's it," Tom said, frowning.

"Yes," Ames replied. "And ever since I heard that, I've been figuring out new security measures for the island. I thought Rotzog's outfit merely intended to try stealing your inventions, but now I'm worried that he means to destroy you!"

Tom was very thoughtful. He also was puzzled. Why wasn't Rotzog worried that another entrant in the rocket race might keep him from realizing his dream of being master of the world? When he expressed this thought aloud, Ames at once said:

"That's easy. You're the only rocket builder who has solved the secret of harnessing the sun's energy to do your work for you. With it, you could be master over this earth."

"No, thanks." Tom's grim look turned to a smile. "There are too many nuts like Rotzog on this planet! I couldn't handle all of them!"

He talked with Ames and Dilling for several minutes about added security measures. It was decided that every plane used by the islanders would carry a ray distorter, an invention of Tom's which had beaten a gang of mysterious pirates. The ray distorter was highly effective against paralyzing supersonic ray guns. The inventor also ordered enough distorters to be set up on the island to shield it completely from aerial attack of this sort.

"I'm going up now in the *Sky Queen* to test the new dual-duty cosmic-ray altimeter and stellar sextant," Tom told his friends. "I'll have a distorter rigged on top of the Flying Lab before it takes off."

Calling the hangar, he told Bud to wait until this was done. An hour later the installation had been made and the giant plane was ready for flight. Tom, Bud, Hanson, and Sterling went aboard. Tom cut in the jet lifters.

The ground vibrated as the enormous craft ascended vertically from the runway. Surging upward with incredible speed, it pierced the early afternoon haze and disappeared from the sight of those on the island.

When the altimeter needle read ten thousand feet, Tom switched to the forward thrust jets and the *Queen* arrowed into a graceful arcing climb.

Putting the plane on gyro pilot, Tom invited the others aft to the laboratory to inspect the instrument he had invented. As they entered, he said:

"This navigational equipment is designed only for the rather short distances that we expect to travel at first. When we really get out into space we'll depend more on the radius indicator."

"How does this invention differ from the ordinary aneroid altimeter that we use now?" Hank Sterling asked.

"An altimeter which depends on measuring atmospheric pressure won't work at very low air pressures," Tom replied. "This instrument picks up the noisy cosmic rays from the sun. The nearer the sun, the noisier the waves."

"How accurate is it?" Hanson asked.

"Within a few feet," Tom replied. "Frankly, this part of the instrument is not my own brain child. The idea has been kicking around for some time."

"You dreamed up the navigation part of it?" Bud asked.

"Yes," Tom answered. "I took the principle of solar radiation and applied it to the stars. This instrument in the black case picks up the waves from three stars and the rocket's position is recorded on the dial—instantly."

"Let's see it work," Hank Sterling urged.

Tom flicked the toggle switch. A whirring sound began and the needle on the dial moved instantly to seventy-eight thousand feet. Another switch was snapped and five dots appeared on the upper dial.

"The black one at the bottom is the earth," Tom explained. "The three red ones are stars."

"The small one must be the fix—the position," Hanson said.

"That's it," Tom replied. "The point of intersection of the lines from the three stars."

"How do you know which stars are showing on your screen?"

"Each first-magnitude star sends its own distinct sound," Tom explained. "Listen."

Three slightly different beeps were coming from the instrument. From a chart Tom identified them as Deneb, Vega, and Altair.

"The greatest feature of this whole thing," Tom continued, "is that the instrument can be built into the automatic pilot."

"You mean," Hanson exclaimed enthusiastically, "that it makes navigation and steering a single operation?"

"That's right," Tom replied.

"Amazing," Hank Sterling commented. "And it certainly appears to be in perfect working order. Tell me, Tom, have you given it a name yet?"

Tom smiled ruefully. "No. I have a harder job naming some of these things than I do figuring them out. Have you any ideas?"

"How about calling it the Spacelane Brain?" Arvid Hanson suggested.

"That sounds like a good name for either the invention or the inventor," Hank spoke up. Then, turning to Tom, he added, "I'm all in favor of it. What do you think, Tom?"

"It sounds good to me," the inventor answered. "The Spacelane Brain it is."

He turned back to his instruments and entered several readings in the log. Without looking up, Tom asked the others if they had noticed the altimeter reading.

"Better than eighty thousand feet," Hanson exclaimed. "You know, this is closer to Heaven than I've ever been!"

"And maybe as close as you'll get, eh?" Hank needled.

Tom grinned and said, "Let's start down."

The trio went back to the pilot's compartment. They had just seated themselves when the *Sky Queen* trembled slightly.

"That's a funny thing to happen all of a sudden!" Bud exclaimed. "It's been smooth flying weather up till now. Not a rough spot the whole way."

"The shock seemed to come from aft," Tom said, "not outside. Do you fellows want to come with me while I investigate?" He looked at Sterling and Hanson. "Bud, keep her on the same heading," he directed his friend.

After checking the panels and seeing that all the jets were okay, the young scientist and his friends retraced their steps aft.

"We'll look in the lab," he said. "The trouble might have originated there."

Tom slid back the heavy door of the soundproofed laboratory. A cloud of sickening fumes poured out into the passageway. Tom recognized them at once.

"It's hydrofluoric acid!" he cried. "I'll get gas masks!"

The acrid fumes were already burning the tissue in his throat as he ran, coughing, to get the masks from a corridor closet.

"Someone must have loosened that acid container," he said to himself as he pulled out the masks. "It never could have spilled otherwise!"

Running back to the laboratory, he handed two masks to his friends and quickly adjusted his own.

"Come on!" he urged. "If we don't neutralize that stuff, it'll eat a hole right through the ship. And if our pressure system fails and our air runs out at this height, we're finished!"

CHAPTER 13

A STARTLING ASCENT

AS TOM RUSHED into the laboratory with Sterling and Hanson, he saw that a large quantity of spilled, fuming acid had already eaten a hole in the floor and penetrated to the lower deck of the plane. It could very well have carried to the vulnerable fuselage!

He dove for a locker, grabbed three packages of slaked lime, and handed one package to Sterling and one to Hanson.

"Sprinkle this around before the whole deck's chewed away!" he shouted through his mask.

Gripping the package, Tom turned and dashed down the passageway to the ladder. He slid open the door to the compartment below and flicked on the light switch. The acid was at work on the floor here too!

But the area it covered was small and Tom quickly poured the neutralizing lime onto the spot. As he

111

watched to be sure the damage had been checked, he wondered how Sterling and Hanson were making out. There was still a possibility that some of the acid had fallen into a crevice in the framework and was eating into the hull.

One thing was sure: The *Sky Queen* must get back to a livable altitude as soon as possible! Rushing to the intercom, he cried:

"Bud, dive to the island as fast as you dare!"

Without asking why, Bud obeyed instantly. As the plane lunged downward, he sensed from Tom's voice that the lives of its occupants depended on his skill.

From the tightness in his stomach and the weightless feeling in his arms, they must be moving about as fast as anyone had ever flown, Tom thought, as the diving speed accelerated.

"What's our altitude?" he asked Bud on the intercom.

"Twenty-eight thousand."

"Still mighty dangerous!" Tom thought. "If the fuselage should spring an air leak—" He closed the door and started for the ladder but grabbed the telephone instead.

"What's it reading now, Bud?"

"Fifteen thousand."

"That's better!" Tom breathed a little more freely in his mask. "Better ease her out of the dive, Bud," he said.

As the *Sky Queen* lost air speed and swept into a graceful downward arc, Tom went to check up on the damage in the laboratory. The slaked lime had done its work well, and a few minutes later the plane settled down on the airstrip.

While the *Sky Queen* was being thoroughly aired, Tom questioned every member of the crew in charge of the big ship to find out how the hydrofluoric acid had become uncapped. He learned that the accident was due to the careless handling of the container by one of the young men while installing it. The man felt so guilty that he offered to resign, but Tom would not hear of it.

"I'm relieved to know that it wasn't sabotage," the young inventor said.

In the meantime, temporary repairs were begun on the Flying Lab. It would be flown to Shopton later for a more complete job.

Toward evening, after the tested altimeter-navigational equipment had been installed in the rocket, Tom received a radiotelephone call from his father.

"Everything okay at home?" Tom asked quickly.

"Yes. Fine. But I've just received news from Washington that is rather disturbing," Mr. Swift said. "One of our rivals is nearly ready to launch his rocket."

"Good night!" Tom cried. "Well, we'll have to speed things up here. Bring Mother and Sandy and the Newtons out to the island day after tomorrow. Bud and I will try to take off at two o'clock."

"Listen, Tom," Mr. Swift said gravely, "I want you to win the rocket race among nations, of course, but not at the risk of your life. Everything must be foolproof before you take off for space!"

"I've seen to that," Tom assured him, "with my anti-G neutralator. And by the way, how is work progressing on the other passenger rockets?"

"On schedule," the older inventor replied. "After your first flight, we'll know whether to make any changes."

Tom immediately called a conference of his top men and relayed his father's message.

"It'll mean extra work to head off this rival Dad speaks of," Tom told them.

"We'll see to it that you're the first one to reach space!" Sterling declared, and there was unanimous agreement on the part of the others. "I know it will depend on how fast we can all pull together," he added. "What do you say, fellows?"

"Let's go!" Hanson urged. "We'll work all night if necessary."

Feverish preparations continued for several hours until Tom called a halt. But everyone was up early the next morning and the work continued. As the noon hour approached, Bud urged Tom to go home with him for lunch and a little rest.

"After my morning's work," he said, "I could eat a whole side of beef topped off with an apple pie."

"If you do, you'll put a lot of excess weight in that rocket," Tom needled him.

To their surprise, it was a fish dinner that Chow set before them. The irrepressible Bud winked at Tom and then began to tease the cook.

"Chow," he said with a sober face, "I take it that you got a new batch of electric eels?"

"No. I caught this here haddock with a lil ole fish pole," he confessed.

Bud feigned a look of disgust. "Chow, you didn't use a rod!"

The cook grinned sheepishly. "Guess I kin do better with an ole fish pole, anyhow. By the way, Tom, has that there rocket o' yours got a name?"

"Yes. It's going to be christened the *Star Spear*. And she's practically ready for orbital flight."

"What does *orbital* mean?" Chow asked, wrinkling his brow.

"Orbital means a track," Tom replied. "A thing to go around on—a more or less circular path."

Bud added, "A rocket in orbital flight is like a baseball swinging at the end of a string. The path of the ball in relation to your fist will be its orbit."

Chow doubled up his fist and swung his arm in a circle. "I get it. Go on."

"In the rocket we turn off the motors at a certain altitude," Tom said, "and keep on flying along our orbit."

"Hm," Chow grunted. "But after you turn off the motors, what's goin' to keep the lil ole rocket goin'?" The cook scratched his bald head. "Why don't she slow down an' tumble right back to the earth?"

"Its centrifugal force exactly balances the pull of the earth," Tom answered. "And there's no mass of air, as we know it here, to interfere with the rocket and slow it down."

"I sure can't figger that," Chow said. "An' you fellows better not count on it either. Take along enough gas to get back!" He turned and left the room.

When the boys finished eating, they hurried back to the launching area, where great tanks of nitric acid and liquid oxygen were being brought alongside the towering rocket.

Technicians were loading camera equipment into the ship. The radarmen were checking the tracking instruments on a high platform near the edge of the area. Tom rode up to the pilot's canopy and installed the tape recorder. He had added a new device. The tape could not only be set to start a flight but would start automatically if the rocket should take off prematurely.

"When do the recording instruments go in?" Bud asked Tom as he returned to the launching platform.

"They're the last thing to be installed," Tom answered. "Members of the Rocket Commission are coming out to see them before the instruments are sealed up and put in the nose. And they're bringing a couple of their own."

As Tom watched in consternation, Bud exclaimed,

Bud wanted to know what still had to be installed before the following afternoon. Tom named several items and said that the most important was his father's dust collector.

"This invention is designed to catch specimens of mineral particles in space that are perhaps not known on earth," Tom explained. "Dad thinks they might be very useful to us."

"How are you going to hold onto this dust at the rate of speed we'll be traveling?" Bud asked.

Tom smiled and said that the dust would be collected on an electrified field between special copper plates arranged just inside a small opening in the rocket's hull.

"Dad has made the plates so

"The rocket ship! It's launched itself!"

foolproof," said Tom proudly, "that the heat from the sun can't fuse the particles to the plates."

Next, Tom went off to inspect the various tanks of fuel before ordering that they be stowed in the four stages of the rocket.

High on the framework, a painter was busy putting on the name. The first word *Star* was finished. As Tom stood gazing at it, Hanson walked up and told him that several of the men wanted to give the two space pioneers a party that evening in honor of the great event.

"Better wait until we've accomplished our mission," the young inventor suggested with a smile.

As soon as Tom and Bud reached their room, they became serious. The enormity of the trip they were about to make took complete possession of their minds and little was said. By morning, however, the boys regained their high spirits and were eager to start.

"If it weren't for the Rocket Commission and the other visitors, we could leave right now," Tom said enthusiastically.

"I suppose we'll need a send-off," Bud replied.

With everything in readiness at nine o'clock, Tom asked Harlan Ames to station himself inside the rocket to prevent any possibility of a last-minute sabotage attempt.

"The *Star Spear* is sealed from this moment," Tom told him. "No one has any authority to come aboard but Bud and myself and anyone with us. The ship is ready to go! Don't recognize any passes. None will apply from now on. Okay?"

"Right!" Ames replied. He stationed two men on the ground while he himself went to the pilot's canopy.

Tom looked at his watch as he stepped off the launcher catwalk. At the same time, an announcement came over the loud-speaker that the Rocket Commission representatives would arrive soon after ten o'clock. The Swifts and Newtons would follow shortly afterward.

"Let's go down to the airstrip and meet them," Tom proposed to Bud.

The boys jumped into a jeep and drove off. They had gone only three hundred yards when from behind them came a strange roar. Tom jammed on the brakes and both boys turned to look.

They stared dumfounded, then gasped in horror.

A gigantic cloud of hot, colored gases was billowing over the launching area. And roaring straight up was a streak against the sky.

"The rocket ship!" Bud exclaimed. "It's launched itself!"

"And Harlan Ames is aboard!" Tom cried fearfully.

CHAPTER 14

EMERGENCY ORDERS

WATCHING in consternation as the rocket ship raced skyward out of control, Tom was unaware for a moment of what had happened on the ground. Now, looking around, he saw men sprawled in various positions. A few started to rise but several, apparently injured, lay still.

"This is terrible!" Bud remarked, his voice barely audible.

Tom nodded as he turned the jeep and rushed back to the scene of the accidental launching. By now the base was in an uproar.

"Bud, take care of those poor fellows," Tom directed. "I'll see what I can do for Ames."

They jumped from the car, and Tom ran to the radar tracking platform where Jones, the operator, stood as if paralyzed with fright. The streaking rocket was already a small speck in the atmosphere. Tom whirled the gun-sight director at it and got an immediate firm fix on the spacebound runaway. Turning to Dilling in the radio shack a few feet away, he shouted:

"Try to contact Harlan Ames. Don't stop trying for a second!"

"Check!" Dilling replied.

"If Harlan only had a chance to flatten himself out during the take-off!" the young inventor murmured hopefully. "Otherwise, he'll be torn to pieces!"

Tom beckoned to the radarman, telling him to switch the tracker from manual to automatic. The giant radar dishes twitched as they aligned themselves to pick up the rocket.

"If Harlan survived the take-off, I'll send him directions on what to do," Tom said.

"What will they be?" Jones asked.

"As soon as we reach Harlan, I'll tell him to cut off the alcohol line to choke the motors of the first three stages, then to dump the liquid oxygen for them."

"Can he do that?" Jones asked.

"Yes, easily," Tom replied. "In that way he won't go up more than a few hundred miles. At least he won't get lost in space!"

A shout sounded in the radio shack. "Tom, Tom! We've reached Ames!" As the young inventor rushed into the shack, Dilling added, "He's in bad shape."

Tom spoke into the transmitter. Giving Ames words of encouragement, he asked him to listen carefully for instructions on how to get back.

"Can you hear me?"

"Yes," came a weak reply.

"Can you move your arms?"

"Yes, a little. Thank heavens your anti-G invention is working. But I think I'm going to black out."

"Hold on for a minute," Tom pleaded, "and you'll be okay."

He then told Ames what buttons to press to cut off the motors and jettison the first three stages.

"Watch your altitude," Tom concluded, "and when the last stage is gone, race the flight tape to the mark for that height on the return trip. It's in green. Roger."

Tom, as well as the others, stood tense and silent. There was a deathlike stillness everywhere in the launching area. Then the receiver crackled three faint words:

"Base stage gone!"

"Thank goodness." Tom breathed a little easier.

Again utter silence. Finally, the welcome announcement was heard that the second stage was dropping through the air with its parachute.

"Third stage released!" said the barely audible voice.

"If Harlan can only reset that flight tape—!" Tom prayed for success, acutely aware that a lag of a few seconds in synchronization would represent the difference between a safe landing and catastrophe. All eyes were riveted on the radarscopes. The pip remained constantly in view. Tom glanced at the tracker to watch the plotting graph as it recorded the return arc of the rocket. Ames was down to a twenty-mile altitude. A few seconds later the reading was only fifteen miles.

"I hope the braking jets have cut in," the young inventor murmured.

"Ames seems to be drifting inland," Jones cried, as the radar dishes swung around so that they were facing westward. "The rocket's not going to land here!"

Tom knew now that Harlan Ames' fate depended on the landing-weight distributor. This invention of Tom's kept the rocket upright if it had to land on a hillside. The tail contained four equidistant magnesium cylinders that extended past the motors to act as supports.

Suddenly the radar contact was gone. "We've lost Ames in the mountains. He must have gone down somewhere in the Adirondacks!" Tom exclaimed.

He took the bearing of the last radar beam and jotted the figures on a scrap of paper. At this moment Bud rushed back to find out what had happened to Ames and to report that none of the injured men was in serious condition.

"Harlan's down. We'll hunt for him. Get the *Sky Queen* ready, will you?" Tom asked Bud. "We'll need several men."

"Okay."

Tom ran to the communications office and got in touch with the head of the New York State Police. After Tom told the chief the advisability of keeping information about the rocket a secret, he agreed to co-operate. His men would hunt for it, take care of Ames, and guard the fallen rocket ship from prying eyes until Tom could get there.

As the young scientist was about to leave, a plane and a high-powered speedboat arrived. The first contained the visitors from Shopton, while the boat discharged members of the Rocket Commission. All were thunderstruck to hear what had happened.

"Have you any idea what set off the rocket?" Mr. Swift asked his son, taking him aside.

"Ames might have started the flight tape accidentally," Tom replied. "But the odds certainly are against that."

"Could it have gone off by itself?" the older inventor suggested. "I thought the safety devices were foolproof."

"They were foolproof," Tom replied in a steady voice, "and errorproof too, but they weren't quite *fiend*proof!"

He took a step closer to his father and said quietly, "The rocket didn't take off because we made any mistake. I'm sure of that. This was a cold-blooded attempt on our lives. I can't be sure how it was done until we can examine the rocket, or talk to Ames—it may be we'll never know. But one of Rotzog's men may have contaminated the alcohol fuel. Or he may have short-circuited the ignition system by remote control, since it's operated electronically."

"That's no doubt the answer," Mr. Swift agreed. "And it's most unfortunate, but I'm confident that Rotzog won't defeat you."

"Thanks, Dad. Now I'd better go find out what I can. Will you show the commissioners around? I'll see you all when I get back. The trip shouldn't take long. And by the way, I think we should keep this top secret if we can, don't you?"

"Yes. We'll stop all outgoing messages from here, and I'll keep everyone on the island until you return. They were expecting to stay until evening, anyway."

Bud had everything ready for the flight when Tom reached the airstrip. Dr. Carman was there, insisting that he wanted to administer to Ames himself.

The *Sky Queen* took off and was put to her greatest speed. A short time later she was cruising over the general area where Tom felt the rocket must have come down. By radio he contacted State Police headquarters and was advised where to look. A report had just come in from a forest ranger that something had hurtled to the ground some miles away from his shack. Bud and the crew combed every inch of woods with binoculars. Suddenly Bud cried out:

"I think I see the rocket standing straight up. Down on the shore of a pond. Yes. There's *Star Spear* painted on the side!"

Fervently hoping its lone occupant was still alive and not badly injured, Tom lowered the great plane to the water and set it down on a broad sandspit at the head of the lake. Everyone hurried out and scrambled up the shore to where the *Star Spear* stood. The rocket seemed to be intact.

Quickly Tom unbolted the flanges on the porthole and crawled through to the pilot's canopy. Dr.

Carman followed. Ames lay on the floor, but the sound of his deep regular breathing assured the others that he was alive. After a hasty examination, the doctor said that the man had suffered nothing more than a bad concussion. In fact, he would "sleep it off."

"When Ames awakens," Dr. Carman went on, "I doubt that he'll remember anything about the trip."

"You mean," Bud said, "that Harlan actually carried out Tom's instructions and didn't know what he was doing?"

"That's my opinion."

The security officer was lifted into the *Sky Queen* and put to bed. Tom heard a crewman say, "It's a miracle!" and Tom had to agree with this observation.

The young inventor directed the transference of the twenty-foot pilot stage into the plane's hangar. As the Flying Lab hovered overhead, cables were looped around the *Star Spear* and it was hoisted aboard.

As the *Sky Queen* started homeward, Tom sent a coded message to Fearing Island giving the latest news. A few minutes went by, then Bud remarked that the plane's course was not a direct one to the island. He questioned his friend about it.

"I'm flying to Shopton," Tom replied with a mysterious smile. "Then Tom Swift Jr. is going to do a little disappearing act."

CHAPTER 15

AN ATTEMPTED THEFT

BUD STARED at Tom. "Well, magician, why are you disappearing and where to?"

For answer, Tom said he believed that it might be a good idea if the Rotzog gang thought he had gone up in the rocket and would not return.

"I do too," Bud agreed. "But you're still going to build another rocket and make the trip, aren't you?"

"Of course. But if our enemies think I've disappeared, they may leave us alone."

"It sure gripes me," said Bud, "to think that now we can't win the rocket race among nations. I suppose we'll only be also-rans."

"Not if I can help it," Tom replied. "The Swift Enterprises and Fearing Island are going to work night and day to complete this project."

"I'm all for it, old-timer," Bud said enthusiastically. "What's my part in this operation?"

"To ferry the sections from the plant."

Tom confided that he felt some deception would be necessary to mislead Rotzog. "I have a stratagem in mind," he added, "but I'll need the Navy's cooperation to make it work."

By this time, the *Sky Queen* was over Shopton. A few minutes later Tom set the plane down on the airfield of the Swift Enterprises plant. He was greeted by a large group of men who had come to ask for full news of the rocket flight.

"So you've heard about it?" Tom remarked.

"All we know," replied an engineer named Walling, "is that several newspapers have been calling here every half-hour to know what's been heard from you. All calls to the island received the answer 'We're not giving out any information.'"

"Good," said Tom. "Next time they phone, tell them it was another test."

"But they think you were in the rocket, Tom," Walling said.

"Let them think so," the young inventor answered. "Give out no information."

He called a meeting of the entire Enterprises engineering personnel, and after telling the full story, pledged them to secrecy. Tom then told of his plan to speed up the assembling of another rocket.

Tom ordered the payload rocket taken from the *Sky Queen* and asked Walling and several other engineers to help him examine the rocket to see if it could be used again. Two hours later the group decided that no damage had been done to the *Star Spear* and that all it required was overhauling.

"When do you think everything will be ready to ship to Fearing?" Tom asked Walling.

"By tomorrow night."

Grinning in anticipation, Tom telephoned the naval station located nearby. Just as he had completed arrangements for assistance, Bud strode into the office.

"Time out for lunch," he announced, bringing in two boxes he had carried over from the cafeteria.

As they ate, Tom said, "If we work fast, we can get all four stages of the rocket to the island tomorrow night while it's still dark."

"Isn't that pretty risky?" Bud asked. "There's a good chance the Rotzog gang will detect that you're running a shuttle to the island."

"I'm not going to fly the sections all the way out," Tom explained.

He revealed the main outline of his plan. The United States Navy had lent him several giant barcs. These amphibious freight trucks were pooled in an isolated field in Fernwood, a tiny village near the coast, across from Fearing Island.

"I'll try to confuse Rotzog by using both the *Sky Queen* and the barcs," Tom said.

"Sounds like a good idea," Bud mused. "Hope it works."

An hour later the Flying Lab and its passengers took off. By the time they arrived at Fearing Island, Harlan Ames was awake and declaring that he felt fine. But as Dr. Carman had prophesied, he recalled nothing of his flight subsequent to the initial take-off.

Ames had been knocked violently to the floor, hitting his head and numbing his arms.

"I didn't start the tape recorder," he answered in reply to a question from Tom. "The rocket just went off all of a sudden as if by magic."

Tom told his suspicions about Rotzog, and Ames whistled.

"He certainly means to destroy you, Tom. But he picked on the wrong guy!"

Arriving at the island, the boys found their guests and the Rocket Commission still there. After dinner, when the commissioners were ready to leave for the mainland, the others strolled to the docks with them. As each man climbed aboard he shook hands with Tom and his father.

The last one, a slender, hatless figure in an old trench coat, was Dr. Herbst, a physics professor from Deland University. He had just started for the boat when the water-front radar alarm system went off. Instantly Tom gripped the surprised professor's arms.

"Mr. Swift, what does this mean?" he exclaimed in a heavy, foreign accent.

Tom's father, equally amazed, could only answer. "I suppose the electronic eye reveals that you have in your possession a metallic object that you were not carrying when you arrived!"

The professor tried to break Tom's grip on his arm. He lunged forward, protesting that he was being dealt with in a most humiliating manner.

"Is this the way you treat guests from the Rocket Commission?" he asked haughtily.

Bud jumped forward and the two boys tightened their hold. They pressed the man into an upright posture.

"I'll report this incident to the newspapers!" he cried. "I've never seen such rudeness. Why, I'll—"

"Just a minute, Professor," Tom retorted. "Maybe the eye made a mistake. We'll forget the alarm. Instead, suppose you just submit to a routine examination. It's possible you've forgotten that you picked up something by mistake."

The physicist stiffened again. His face whitened with rage as he sensed the ruse. Nevertheless he said:

"Very well, then. As long as this is just routine."

The boys released their hold and took a step back from Dr. Herbst. Instantly the man flashed his right hand under his jacket lapel, pulled out a small shiny object, and flung it far out into the bay!

"You won't find out what it was!" the professor cried vindictively.

Tom glanced at the other members of the Rocket Commission. They were speechless with astonishment.

Bud Barclay, who had watched intently as the object hit the water, instantly shed his coat and kicked off his moccasins. Then he dived from the dock. An underwater crawl stroke carried him in a matter of seconds directly to the place where the object had disappeared.

On the dock, the professor was protesting his innocence. Tom and his father had taken hold of him again and he was fuming just as he had been a moment before.

"What was that object you threw out there?" Mr. Swift demanded.

"It was my own!" Herbst argued. "My personal property! I was afraid you'd confiscate my invention. It's a secret one I didn't want revealed!"

For a moment the man wore a look of triumph. But his expression changed suddenly as Bud appeared on the surface with his right hand thrust up out of the water. He was clenching something in his hand.

Bud swam to the dock, then climbed the ladder and handed the object to Tom.

"It's your new high-powered transistor," Bud said.

"What!" Mr. Swift cried. "Why, this is the most important part of your computer!"

Tom clutched the transistor and turned to Herbst. "Well, Professor, what have you got to say?" he demanded.

Completely shaken by the unexpected turn of events and the stares of his colleagues in the boat, Herbst suddenly collapsed. When he recovered from the shock, he submitted to questioning without protest.

He told the Swifts that a countryman of his had looked him up shortly after his appointment to the Rocket Commission. Innocently, at first, Herbst had revealed to him information about the rocket projects he had visited. His countryman had then persuaded him that it was his patriotic duty to gather as much secret data as he could get from Fearing Island, and, if possible, key parts.

"Patriotism hardly requires you to stoop so low as to steal from a fellow scientist," Mr. Swift said icily. "What is the name of your fellow countryman who is responsible for this outrage?"

"I'm in fear of my life to tell," replied the man nervously. "I still have relatives in my own country and I was warned to keep silent—or else harm might come to them."

"We have no choice but to turn you over to the FBI. But it will go a lot easier with you if you confess."

The dejected man sat motionless for a few moments, staring at the floor of the boat. Then he looked up and said:

"The man who is responsible for this is called Rotzog."

"How long have you known him?" Tom asked.

"I don't know him at all," Herbst replied. "I was approached by a Mr. Hein. He seems to be some sort of henchman."

"We know about him," said Tom quietly. "Did he ever mention where the outfit's rocket-launching area is?"

"Then you know about the Rotzog group?" the professor asked in amazement.

"Yes."

"I know very little about the Rotzog rocket and I have no idea where it is. Please believe me," Herbst pleaded.

Tom and his father looked at each other and nodded. On the last point they agreed that the professor was telling the truth. He was taken away to await the arrival of an agent from the Federal Bureau of Investigation.

The rest of the Rocket Commission, almost too astounded to comment about their traitorous associate, rode off in the speedboat. Soon afterward, the other visitors left and the islanders settled down to a peaceful evening.

An hour later, however, the calmness was broken by news brought by an FBI agent. A large New York evening paper had carried a scoop saying one of their reporters had been tipped off that Tom Swift Jr. had been lost in a rocket launched prematurely.

"Good night!" the young inventor exclaimed. "Who gave out such a story?"

Harlan Ames said he would check its source. In a call to the city editor the security agent learned that a reporter in New York had picked up the tip from a foreigner near International Airport.

"If we want to find out more about the story," Ames said, "this reporter, Al Landry, will meet us at International in New York."

"I'm on my way!" Bud cried.

CHAPTER 16

OPERATION SHUTTLE

FLYING a speedy jet, Bud took off with Harlan
Ames for New York. Upon arriving at International
Airport, the security man pointed out the hatless reporter who was waiting for them. Landry turned out
to be a jovial young ex-football player who covered
the airport news for his paper.

He introduced his companion as Hjalmar Koos
and explained, "Mr. Koos is a language expert, who
may be able to help us. He speaks fifteen languages.
The man I talked to about Swift's rocket ship ought
to speak one of 'em! If not, we'll get Koos' brother
who knows the other fifteen!" he joked.

Koos smiled as Landry went on to explain, "This
mustached fellow I mentioned has been coming to a
quiet restaurant near here at ten o'clock each night.
He always meets one or two men and they speak in a
language I don't understand. But off and on, when
they speak English, I've picked up stories from them

135

about other foreigners they seem to know. Since you're so much interested in these fellows, I thought Koos might eavesdrop on what they say among themselves in their own tongue.''

"Say, it's almost ten o'clock now," Bud broke in excitedly. "Let's head for that restaurant."

By the time the three reached the place, they had settled on a plan of action. Koos was to remain outside until after the stranger entered and had been pointed out. Bud, Ames, and Landry obtained a booth, with Landry keeping out of sight.

A few minutes later a mustached man appeared at the door, and as Bud glanced questioningly at the reporter, he nodded slightly.

"That's the one!" Landry whispered.

The man walked to another booth and in a moment a waiter brought him coffee and buns. Presently another man, tall and heavy-set, entered the restaurant. At a nod from Landry, Koos followed close behind and seated himself at a table only a few feet from the foreigners' booth. As before, the waiter brought buns and coffee to the second stranger. Koos ordered the same.

Bud suggested to Ames that they follow the men when they left. But Landry tried to dissuade him.

"You'd better wait and hear what Koos has to say before you get into trouble."

Bud agreed that it was sound advice, but planned to be ready to leave at a moment's notice. He ordered a sandwich and milk.

It was only a matter of minutes before the suspect

pair rose and left. Koos immediately headed for Bud's table.

"I understood them all right," he began in a low voice. "The one who came in first was very happy because the Swifts had not denied the story he had given Landry. He feels sure Tom really was in the lost rocket!

"The big fellow," Koos went on, "told the other that Rotzog thinks he can smash any American effort to launch a rocket, now that Tom Swift Jr. is gone!"

"What!" Bud cried, sliding out of the booth so fast he knocked over his empty milk glass.

With Ames at his heels, Bud rushed outside to question the Rotzog men further. But they were not in sight. Bud concluded that the two had ridden off in a car which was traveling down the street at a fast clip. Realizing that he and Ames could not overtake it in traffic, Bud returned to the restaurant with his friend.

Landry was sorry that he had kept them from contacting the suspects but promised to find out all he possibly could the next evening. He would let Bud know what he learned.

Before leaving the restaurant, Bud asked the owner if he were acquainted with the foreigners, but the man shook his head. One bit of information he did tell about them was discouraging. The men had mentioned to him that they would not be back—they were leaving New York permanently. Bud was disheartened, and as he and Ames flew back to Fearing Island, he said:

"I hope Tom has better luck tomorrow night than we've had tonight."

Reaching the island, Bud related what had happened. Tom, instead of being downcast about the two suspects not being caught, said:

"Anyway, I'm still among the missing." He grinned. "And I'll stay there until you and I return from our rocket race."

Early the next evening Tom flew with Bud to Shopton where the four stages of the new rocket were ready for transporting. Tom and his father were to ride with Bud in the *Sky Queen* to carry the payload stage to Fernwood and stay with it. Then Bud, Arvid Hanson, and the crew would shuttle the plane and move the other three sections there one by one.

After the cabin end of the *Star Spear* had been loaded into the hangar of the Flying Lab, the gigantic plane headed for the little seashore village of Fernwood. Twenty minutes later it hovered in mid-air, several miles from the small hamlet, where there was a fleet of outsized amphibious barcs parked along a lonely road. These were sixty-ton amphibious cargo carriers, almost wide enough to touch both curbs of a normal street. Their wheels stood ten feet high.

Bud set the *Sky Queen* down to a point about five feet above one of the tremendous wheeled boats. The rocket section was lowered into the barc with a single motion and covered with a tarpaulin.

Tom and Mr. Swift, hats pulled down, climbed

onto the operator's seat next to the driver. The monster marine truck rolled toward the bay.

The barc continued along the road for a mile out to the ocean beach. Mr. Swift saw, to his surprise, that several Navy enlisted men and officers were grouped on the shore. Some of them climbed onto the vehicle before its square prow pushed into the bay. The craft carried its load with ease, picking up speed as it moved away from land.

The men introduced themselves and one of the officers said to Mr. Swift, "Pretty neat strategy your boy's pulling off here."

Mr. Swift smiled. "Yes, it is!"

About half a mile dead ahead was a brightly lighted Navy auxiliary ship lying at anchor. Great clusters of cargo lights hung about the booms, casting reflections out across the waves.

"What's going on here, Tom?" Mr. Swift whispered, as the Navy men left the barc to climb aboard the big ship.

"The ship is just a ruse," Tom replied. "We're not delivering anything to her. This is an old Navy trick. Empty barcs have been running out to the ship since eleven o'clock last night."

The lights on the ship were suddenly dimmed. The barc slid past it in the darkness and headed for Fearing Island. On the shore of the island metal tracks had been put down to keep the carrier from becoming mired. When the barc reached land, the giant tires rolled onto the tracks and the heavily weighted craft lumbered ashore.

The main section of the Star Spear *was safe!*

"Here comes the next section!" Tom cried presently. "Bud's really got everyone on the *Queen* hustling."

As they started toward the beach to meet the barc, Tom and his father were startled by a scream, then a cry from the cove.

"Help! Help!"

CHAPTER 17

AN IMPORTANT CAPTURE

"THAT SOUNDS like Chow!" Tom said as the call for help was repeated.

He and his father climbed aboard a jeep that had been left parked nearby and raced in the direction of the cove. They sped past the boys' cottage and down to the dunes.

Mr. Swift and Tom jumped out and ran to the water's edge. In the glow from the car's headlights they could see vaguely a battle going on between two figures inside Chow's weir. One was a man, the other a strange-looking creature. First one was knocked under water, then the other.

"That's Chow!" Tom cried suddenly. "But what's the other thing?"

The Swifts stood by, ready to assist if necessary. In a few seconds, however, they smiled as the Texan came off the victor, dragging his opponent onto the beach.

"Man alive, what have you got there?" Tom asked. Chow's prisoner was a man but presented a very strange appearance. He was covered from shoulders

"That's Chow!" Tom cried suddenly

to feet in a tight-fitting, one-piece suit of rubberized fabric and wore a glass faceplate, connected by a length of one-inch tubing to two metal cylinders that were strapped to his back.

"I sure don't know what I picked up," Chow said, shaking his head.

"This," Tom explained to him, "is a frogman costume of extremely advanced design. If we look in the water out there, I believe we'll find a propeller-driven underwater craft that this fellow used to get here."

"You don't suppose he's got a bomb with him, do

you, Tom?" Chow asked excitedly. "I remember readin' about rigs like this bein' used to blow up ships."

"He may have," Tom answered, "although I doubt it. But I'll bet that when we search him, we'll find something a good deal more interesting."

By this time the intruder had removed his helmet. Tom said to the stocky dark-haired frogman:

"What's your name? And what are you doing here?"

"My name's Will Ward, and you can see for yourself what I was doing. I came out from the mainland farther than I thought. I was getting pretty tired, so I decided to land and rest for a while. There's nothing wrong with that, is there? Now if you're finished, I'll leave."

"I'm afraid you can't leave until we've had a better look at you, and you've answered a few more questions," interjected Mr. Swift. "This is a restricted area and you have been trespassing. You'd better come along with us."

Will Ward stood defiantly where he was for a few seconds. Then, realizing that escape was impossible under the circumstances, he fell in with his captors and marched up to the security office. They were met by Harlan Ames, whose eyes widened at the sight of the interloper. As Ames took the man in tow to supply him with other clothes, Tom's father quietly asked his son:

"What do you make of this, Tom?"

"I think that man is Marvin Hein!" Tom announced. "He fits the description to a T that Asa Pike gave us up in Hankton. I think he's here to sabotage our rocket, and he chose the one way to get here that would avoid detection by both our radar and sonar defenses. It was just pure luck for us that he happened to swim into Chow's fishing weir."

"You mean I really caught a big fish, after all?" Chow exclaimed jubilantly. "Well, you sure got to thank my new 'lectric eels what you sent for, Tom. I was cartin' 'em down to the water, when what do I see in my flashlight but that critter flounderin' around in my trap. I figgered he sure didn't have no business there."

The Swifts smiled, then Mr. Swift became serious. "It's my opinion our visitor may have entered the country illegally," he said. "We'll suggest to the police that he be held on suspicion."

Within a few minutes Ames returned with a small flat metal case to which were attached four coils of thin insulated wire.

"Look what I found on Ward," he said, and handed the box to Tom.

The two inventors examined it. "Just as I thought," Tom said excitedly. "This is a relay circuit with a built-in timing device to ignite the *Star Spear* prematurely, after it had been fueled. This is probably how the rocket was set off when Ames was aboard. Once connected in place, it would be a cinch to hide this thing."

"The box itself," Mr. Swift remarked, "has a tiny distorter on it so our radar couldn't pick up the device. After the frogman was safe on land, he'd remove the distorter." Grimly he laid a hand on his son's shoulder. "Tom, I believe your life and Bud's have been spared. This stranger intended to put this device in your new rocket ship."

Tom turned to Chow. "I have you to thank for

thwarting our enemies' latest plot against us," he said.

The cook beamed, then became angry. "Let me get my hands on that sneakin' frog of a man!" He started out the door.

"That won't be necessary," Tom said, grabbing Chow's arm. "The authorities will take care of him."

Tom, accompanied by his father, Ames, and Chow, went to the room where the visitor was being detained. After the Swifts had revealed to him how much they knew, the man finally confessed that he was Marvin Hein. He had been on Fearing Island once before and installed the relay circuit in Tom's first rocket ship.

"But this is all I will admit," Hein continued. "I am pledged not to betray my leader!"

"Do you mean your country—as well as your leader?" Tom asked.

"I mean only my leader—Rotzog!" Hein replied. "He is the world's greatest scientist. He will build the first space platform and rule the world. Nobody can stop him!"

"Except Tom Swift Jr.!" exclaimed Chow, who was gloating over his part in the affair. "Tom's goin' to be the first fellow to get up among them planets an' win that there world-wide rocket race. An' nobody's goin' to stop *him!*"

Hein lapsed into stony silence and was removed to the mainland to be held on suspicion.

"But where Rotzog and his rocket are hidden still remains a secret," Tom told his father.

"Don't be discouraged," Mr. Swift advised. "I'd say all the breaks so far have been on your side. They've failed to hold anyone from your group and you've captured five of their men!"

Tom grinned. "Rotzog's next!"

The young inventor went off to meet Bud who was just coming in with the final rocket section. As Bud climbed down, Tom slapped him on the back.

"A swell job, fellow."

His husky friend grinned. "That was a neat operation you dreamed up, shuttle boy, but I sure feel like a worn-out ferryboat."

As the boys walked to their quarters, Tom told about Hein's capture.

Bud whistled. "So Rotzog has stopped sending small boys to do a man's errand. Now he sends his top men, eh?"

Tom was serious. "He might have wrecked this place," he remarked. "I've ordered a day-and-night patrol of the beaches in addition to our alarm system."

At eight o'clock the next morning the boys went directly to the launching area, where engineers had already started to assemble the replacement rocket. As soon as Tom was satisfied that the work was progressing satisfactorily he sought out his father.

"Dad, shall we rig up your dust collector now?"

This was the device which would gather bits of cosmic mineral matter. Mr. Swift believed that it would be of great value to scientists. The elder inventor shook his head.

"The dust collector doesn't open automatically. I'm trying a new type of shutter on it. I'll contact you when the apparatus is ready to be installed in the *Star Spear.*"

"Okay, Dad."

Tom went to his own laboratory where he replaced the cathode-ray tube in the oscillograph with another one which he knew to be more sensitive. As Bud walked in with Chow, he winked at Tom and said:

"At ten G's you and I will each weigh a ton."

The cook looked at the boys suspiciously, then said, "Say, Tom, what are these lil ole G's you all talk about? They sure got me bothered. It ain't natural. Sounds like gangster talk or the FBI."

Tom laughed at the way the puzzled cook wrinkled his forehead. "Sorry, Chow, you're wrong on both counts. The term G is a unit of measure, like a pound of something or a dollar."

"Of which I have too much of the first an' not enough of the other—at least till payday!" Chow sighed.

"The G factor measures the basic attraction the earth has for a unit mass at the earth's surface," Tom continued. Then, smiling at Chow, he went on, "Now in your case, Chow, you have more mass than Bud or I, so the earth loves you more than it does us, and hangs on to you tighter."

Chow snorted and said, "It kin hang onto me just as tight as it wants—the tighter the better!"

Tom and Bud laughed, and Tom resumed his explanation.

"Someday, Chow, bring a bathroom scale down to the plant and put it in the elevator. Weigh yourself, then press the button for the top floor.

"The faster the elevator starts, the more you weigh. Now, if the scale reading was twice as much as it was when you were standing still that would be a force of two G's. When the *Star Spear* takes off, Bud and I may weigh ten times as much as we do right now—that would be a force of ten G's."

"I catch your meanin'," Chow admitted. "An' I *know* I sure better stay here. I weigh too much already!" He laughed jovially. "Well, since I ain't fixin' to test how many G's a lil ole outer-space flapjack kin handle, there's no use o' this old cowpoke goin' with you."

After the chef had left the laboratory, Bud said, "What's next on the schedule?"

"Checking our space suits and fortifying the island still further."

Bud looked up in amazement. "Fearing's an electronic arsenal now. Even a vulture would fly for his life from this place!"

"But Rotzog is one bird who won't," Tom pointed out. "I'm installing a second group of robot jets to circle about those drones that are up there now."

"Sounds like action and I'm all for it!" Bud said enthusiastically. "Come on!"

CHAPTER 18

ZERO-HOUR INTERRUPTION!

THREE ROBOT JETS were loaded into the hangar of the *Sky Queen* and the great door was closed. Bud, at the controls, lifted the plane to ten thousand feet as Tom had directed.

"Check!" Bud telephoned to his waiting friend.

Tom clicked the button that opened the door, then sparked the first drone by remote control. It shot out into the atmosphere. The young inventor smiled as the perfectly calibrated automaton instantly began its circling pattern.

As it swept under him on its return flight, Tom released the second drone, and a few seconds later the third. They followed the others in faultless rhythm.

"Okay," Tom reported. When the door was shut, he said, "We'll go back for the other three jets."

"Roger."

After the second set of robots had taken their

places in the two-mile-high protection area, Tom joined Bud in the pilots' cabin.

"Operation Down-to-Earth," Bud said, "is becoming more hazardous all the time. I'd hate to hit one of these robots and have it blow up in my face!"

As Tom watched his friend skillfully take down the *Sky Queen*, he remarked, "Rotzog is clever. I hope he can't find a way to break our barrier before we launch the rocket. I'll feel much safer when I'm four hundred miles up."

"What's your real opinion of that guy's aims?" Bud asked. "Do you believe what his men said about him?"

"I'm convinced," Tom answered, "that Rotzog is a modern kind of Alexander or Napoleon, or even a Hitler. But instead of trying to conquer the earth, he's hoping to become master of all space. I think he has a nearly completed space station that he's going to launch in sections, then go up to assemble them."

"But he can't do it unless he has the right fuel," Bud remarked. "If Johnson didn't get enough information about the kicker when he was snooping in your lab, to pass it along to Rotzog, maybe he isn't ready."

"I have an idea we'll soon know," Tom replied. "When we launch the *Star Spear*, Rotzog will come after us. Better keep this top secret, Bud, or there may be objections to our leaving."

"My lips are sealed, Tom." Bud grinned. "I'm just itching for a good old game of tag in space. And by the way," he added, "the sooner we get launched, the less likelihood there'll be of one of our legitimate rivals beating us in the race. Any more news of the rival rocket that was supposed to take off pretty soon?"

"I'll check when we land."

It took over an hour to acquire the information. When it came, Tom was alarmed. One of the rockets in the international race was to be launched in the center of Australia at nine A.M. the day after tomorrow."

"That's six P.M. tomorrow here!" Bud exclaimed.

"Right! Bud, we're going to leave tomorrow afternoon!"

Ames, who was standing nearby, stared in astonishment. "Can you be ready by that time?"

In reply, Tom broadcast the word over the loudspeaker system, asking for an immediate report on the status of the *Star Spear*. One by one the answers trickled in.

"Entire electric system checked."

"Motors in perfect time."

"Fuel ready to be piped in."

So it went, with only minor details to be attended to. Fearing Island hummed during the balance of the day, with every worker confident that Tom Swift's rocket would win the race.

The young inventor telephoned to his mother asking that she and Sandy come for the launching.

Next, he called the Newton home, then got in touch with the head of the Rocket Commission. Each group promised to arrive during the morning.

These details attended to, Tom and Bud now tried on the space suits which would be carried in case of emergency. They had been constructed from a tightly woven wire fabric of extremely high bursting strength. The suits were covered on each side with an impermeable layer of a new synthetic rubber, jointed together to permit movement, and were absolutely airtight.

Encased in these effective but clumsy garments, the boys would be able to survive exposure to the space void for a period of several hours, should a chance collision with one of the hundred thousand meteorites which fall to the earth daily damage the *Star Spear*.

"Let's hope we don't have to put the suits on," Tom said to Bud. "I want to win that race in the *Star Spear!*"

"Right! See you later." Bud went off to place the space suits in lockers reserved for them.

Tom's next move was to install another vital safety feature in the *Star Spear*—a spare kicker. The present one might become poisoned by a trace of impure oxygen. But to make the replacement, Tom decided he would have to substitute improved couplings which would permit him to insert the new kicker in a matter of seconds. While doing this, it would be necessary to by-pass the kicker and use the main fuel line. This operation would consume huge quantities of the precious fuel and could not be kept up long.

"Repairs will have to be done with split-second timing," the young inventor said to himself.

Hours later he was satisfied with his work. Accompanied by several engineers, he went up to the payload stage where they installed the new couplings and fastened down the emergency kicker.

It had already grown dark when the job was finished. As the men descended to the ground, Tom saw Chow waiting for him. Good old Chow! He was going to see that the boys did not forget to eat!

The Texan served what Bud termed a lollapalooza of a meal and Tom declared that he would not have to eat again before going around the world!

When the boys returned to the launching area, trucks were already arriving from the storage tanks with their loads of fuel. Tom and Bud watched the procedure. Presently Tom glanced up and saw the noselights of the circling drones. He thought he detected another sound from high above them. As he listened, another fuel truck moved toward the launching area. Tom was joined by Hank Sterling at the base of the rocket.

"I thought—" Tom began, but he never finished the sentence.

A bright flash had appeared suddenly in the dark sky, near the upper defense circle. Then there was another brilliant burst of light, just above the first.

A second later two jarring explosions rocked the

island. The sirens started wailing. The floodlights flared on.

But even their intense glare failed to blot a blinding flash overhead as one of the low-level drones exploded. It blew to pieces directly over the airstrip, showering the rocket area with fragments.

Fires broke out in a dozen places at once!

CHAPTER 19

SEALED INSTRUMENTS

"ALL FIRE EQUIPMENT OUT!" Tom yelled
over the tracking platform's loud-speaker. "And
turn off the floodlights!"

The watchman on duty in the power shack dashed
to the control board and threw the master switch.
As the island plunged into darkness, patches of fire
burned brightly in a dozen or more places on and
within the buildings.

The biggest blaze was roaring along the truck
road where the loaded vehicles had been abandoned
because of the explosions. Tom noticed the peculiar
lasting way in which the flames burned on the
ground and knew instantly what it meant.

"Bud!" he exclaimed. "This stuff is jellied gaso-
line! Napalm bombs have been dropped on us!"

A fire engine ground to a stop near the rocket.
Its crew leaped into action, shooting chemicals upon
the lively flames that threatened the *Star Spear*.

Tom grabbed two portable extinguishers from the fire truck and handed them to Hank Sterling and Bud.

"Follow me!" he yelled, removing one more from the apparatus and starting to run toward the truck road. The others raced along behind him.

"We've got to keep the flames away from the tank trucks!" Tom cried. "If the loaded ones blow up, we're done for!"

In the flickering light of the flames that seemed almost to touch the vehicles, the three could see a pumping engine working frantically in the area ignited by the exploding tanks. The truck drivers, who had fled to temporary safety, now returned to assist in quenching the flames.

Tom, Bud, and Hank ran toward three giant trucks which were dangerously exposed to the terrific heat of the spreading fire.

"You take the first one!" Tom yelled to Hank. "Bud and I will take the others!"

A hundred yards beyond, both sides of a second vehicle were threatened by flames. Bud leaped into the cab, and with Tom hanging on, drove the truck forward another hundred yards, ending the immediate danger.

Tom jumped off and ran to the last truck that had just left the storage tanks when the explosion occurred. Only seconds remained in which to save it, because a blob of napalm had fallen on the hood from which the fire threatened to engulf the cab.

The guard at the storage tanks had stuck to his

The crew leaped into action, shooting chemicals

post and a heavy spray was sweeping over the entire section, dousing the fuel containers with fire-fighting chemical. But should the truck explode, flying pieces of metal from it could pierce a tank like shrapnel and release the highly inflammable contents.

Reaching the truck, Tom decided on a bold move. He would back the flaming truck into the storage area within range of the extinguishers there. Shielding his eyes with his arm, Tom leaped into the cab, and with a prayer, pressed the starter button, slammed the truck into reverse, and roared backward down the road for thirty yards to where the extinguisher nozzles were emitting foaming chemicals.

Soon the flames that had come so close to devastating the island were entirely under control. The

upon the flames that threatened the Star Spear

rocket remained intact and the supply of the special fuels, to be used for the flight into space, was saved.

Dr. Carman was kept busy for an hour attending to minor burns and treating the stinging eyes of several men. At last all those not on duty for the night retired to their quarters.

In the meantime Tom, Bud, and Hank had rushed back to the rocket ship to see if its sensitive instruments had suffered any damage. A thorough checkup assured them that everything was in perfect working order. The attack had failed!

"It's mighty lucky you launched the upper defense drones!" Tom's father remarked as they finished their inspection.

"How many of them did we lose?" Tom asked the control-tower operator.

"Three of the top level and one of the regulars," the operator replied. "But I hate to think what would have happened if they hadn't stopped most of the bombs from dropping straight through!"

A few moments later the all-clear signal sounded and again the trucks took up their work. By four A.M. the fueling operation had been completed without further interruption and the weary boys turned in for a few hours' rest.

"You know, Tom, the peace and quiet of outer space is going to come as a welcome relief after the goings on around here," Bud said to his pal as they stretched out in their beds. "Rotzog has tried about everything on us but germ warfare. Do you suppose we'd better start boiling our drinking water tomorrow?"

"I wouldn't put that past him, either," Tom replied with a grim smile. "He'd resort to such tactics. But," he added resolutely, "I don't intend to give our enemies enough time to strike again."

"Glad to hear that!" Bud gave a tremendous yawn and a minute later both boys were sound asleep.

As dawn broke, the blinker on Fearing Island's short-wave system suddenly flashed on the black panel in the communications office. When no one answered, a buzzer sounded. George Dilling leaped from his bunk in the next room to switch on the set.

The caller was Radnor, the security assistant, who, upon being released from the hospital, had gone to Washington to confer with the FBI and other authorities on the progress of the hunt for Rotzog and his rocket base.

"At last! At last!" came his excited but faraway voice. "I'm up in the Aleutians in a search plane. We've got news of Rotzog's hide-out!"

"Go on!" Dilling urged.

Radnor's voice was not coming through clearly. It would fade, strengthen, and fade again. Dilling strained his ears to put the message together.

"We're on our way to check on a report a fisherman brought in a few minutes ago," the agent continued. "The man tells us that he saw a giant rocket on a lonely island five days ago. It's taken him all this time to get the news to us by boat. Almost a thousand miles of open sea."

"What's the location?" Dilling asked.

"We have the fisherman here in the plane," Radnor replied. "We should arrive at the spot within an hour and a half. We'll call you. But get word to Tom that he mustn't delay. Rotzog will be a worse menace than ever if he should get away from us. He may even pick up our plane on his radar and zoom off. Our skipper figures we'll flush him out, because if he doesn't belong on the island he'll leave in a rush. So tell Tom to hurry! Over!"

Dilling was tempted to reveal Tom's plans for taking off but kept silent. He switched off the set and buzzed Tom's telephone. Already awake, Tom answered.

"What is it?" he asked. After being told the news, he exclaimed, "I must take off immediately!"

Bud already was on his feet. "We'd better get everyone up!" he cried, and Tom nodded.

He gave the orders and dressed quickly. Within an hour the entire base was in action. Trucks carrying last-minute emergency items were unloading at the catwalk. Water and rations were being put aboard.

Mr. Swift hurried to Tom's side on the launching platform. "Mother and Sandy ought to be here any minute," he said anxiously.

"I certainly wouldn't want to leave without saying good-by to them," Tom said. "The Rocket Commissioners promised to be here at nine, and we can't take off before then, anyway."

Looking up suddenly at two incoming planes, he said, smiling, "They're both arriving ahead of schedule."

When the planes landed, the groups were amazed

to hear that the time for the launching had been moved up. Mrs. Swift was very quiet and Tom knew she was fighting tears. He put his arm around her.

"Don't worry, Momsy," he said, using his childhood name for her. "I'll be back before you get used to my being away."

"Be careful, son, and good luck," she managed to answer. Then, with a faint smile, she added, "We'll meet you in San Francisco. You know I don't like speed, but the *Sky Queen* is going to make the West Coast in less than two hours so we can be there when you come down."

Chow, who had been standing by, lifted his eyebrows. "Well, brand my geography lessons, I thought you were figurin' on goin' clean 'round the world, Tom—not landin' a couple o' thousand air miles or more from here."

"I'll circle the globe, all right," Tom said. "But don't forget that while I'm traveling, the earth will be turning at the rate of over a thousand miles an hour."

"You mean," the cook asked, "that in a little while San Francisco will be here?"

"That's about it. So actually Bud and I will start and stop at this point."

Chow consulted his watch and grinned. "We been expressin' along for several miles while we been standin' still an' talkin'?"

"Sure thing, Chow."

Tom now told his family and the three Newtons that he had arranged for the rocket to be christened and had chosen his mother to perform the honors.

"Since it wouldn't be safe for you to get close to the *Star Spear* at the time of launching and break the traditional bottle on it," he said, "I've arranged something else. There's a certain button on the tracking platform for you to push. By remote control it will uncover the name and the symbol on the *Star Spear*."

Everyone expressed surprise about the symbol which had been added during the night and hidden by a magnetic disk.

"I've read," Tom went on, "that originally the bottles broken against the prows of ships about to be launched contained waters from the seven seas. My symbol represents the seven large stars of the Pleiades, where I hope to fly some day."

Tom did not reveal any more, and though his listeners were curious, they refrained from asking questions.

"I'll be very happy to christen your rocket ship, Tom," his mother said. "What do you want me to do?"

Tom led Mrs. Swift to the platform and showed her the special button she was to touch after the announcer called, "Minus one!" "And I believe," he added, "that minus one will be at ten o'clock."

Hearing his name called at this moment, Tom left her and went to speak to the three members of the Rocket Commission. They had come to seal their recording instruments in the nose section. Without these official proofs, Tom's flight would not be recognized by the international judges. The head representative, a tall, dignified man, aware that time was short, swung onto the conveyor and zoomed up to the nose section. Hurriedly Mr. Hopkins checked the tiny wires which had been threaded through the recording instruments, and then sealed the ends together through a soft metal slug by means of special pliers. It would now be impossible to open the instruments without detection.

Returning to the ground, Mr. Hopkins said to Tom, "The instruments are set. On behalf of the Rocket Commission I wish you a successful flight!"

As he turned away, Tom looked at Bud.

"Ready?"

"Check."

The two boys shook hands with all the men and in return received pats on the back and wishes of Godspeed. Hank Sterling said, "Win that prize!" Arvid Hanson whispered, "Watch out for Rotzog. He's not in the race, but he may still try to ruin you!"

Chow added, "Give my regards to them Martians an' find out what they eat up there!"

"I'll guard this island with my life while you're gone, Tom," Ames promised.

Tom and Bud now kissed Mrs. Newton, Phyl, Sandy, and Mrs. Swift good-by. They all wished the adventurers well, but as Tom's mother walked to the tracking platform he could see that she was trembling.

Tom bade his father farewell last of all. There was a long, firm handclasp as silent messages were conveyed from the eyes of each. Finally Mr. Swift said:

"I'm proud that you are carrying on my work so admirably."

Tom and Bud entered the rocket and rode the conveyor belt to the pilot's canopy. When the conveyor was removed, the openings through the center of each stage were sealed off one by one from the control cabin.

Tom now radioed to the radar tracking level. "Sweep a 360-degree circle with the dishes. We're going up in less than a minute if all is clear. Pay attention to the high level. If there's any danger it will strike above five hundred miles."

"Okay!" Jones called back.

The battery of gleaming radar screens began moving in silent, fantastic patterns. For fifteen seconds they swept the skies in every direction.

"Sky's clear!" came the report.

"Has the launching area been evacuated?" Tom asked.

"All clear below!"

"Here goes!" said Tom.

He set the flight tape in action, then quickly the boys flattened themselves on the slanting take-off racks and buckled the safety straps.

The tape set off the time clock and the loudspeakers in the cabin, and on the launching platform a voice boomed out:

"*X minus ten!*"

"Sure your straps are tight?" Tom asked Bud tensely.

Across the cabin his friend gave a tug and nodded. "Won't be long now," Bud said. "Good luck, pal!"

"—coming X minus five—minus four—minus three—

The boys held their breaths. Tom kept his eyes glued on the tape.

"Minus one!"

Down below, the forefinger of Mrs. Swift's right hand pushed a small button. At once the name and the symbol on the rocket were revealed. Between the two words a bright red spear was piercing a seven-pointed white star. Alongside the lowest triangle on the right were the initials U.S.A. lighted up in red, white, and blue.

The watchers saw all this in a split second. Then there was a gigantic puff of billowing gases and the *Star Spear* began to lift.

A few seconds later Tom Swift's rocket ship was on its journey into space!

CHAPTER 20

GHOST WINDS

THE ROCKET SHIP shivered as the blast hurtled it off the ground. Tom and Bud felt their bodies flatten against the racks as the enormous acceleration forces caught them in a viselike grip.

"What power!" Bud murmured, as he slid his rack over to a porthole window and glanced down at the receding ground.

Out across the Atlantic the clouds, in reality drifting at eight thousand feet, appeared to hover just above the waves like a mist. The horizon was already sloping off, giving the earth a mound shape.

"Check time!" Dilling radioed.

"Sixteen seconds and we've reached the ionosphere!"

Suddenly the rocket was jarred by a violent movement. The abrupt motion nearly wrenched the boys from their racks.

"Hey!" Bud cried. "We must have collided with something!"

"Whatever it is, hang on!" Tom exclaimed, as the rocket ship gave a sharp twist.

The boys had just managed to grip the sides of their acceleration couches when the rocket, already traveling straight up at 4500 miles an hour, gave an even more violent lurch.

"Tom!" gasped Bud. "What's happened to us?"

As the huge rocket shuddered under this latest impact, Tom and Bud clung tenaciously to their racks.

"We—we must be—caught in one of—those jet streams!" Tom managed to say between the violent motions.

"You mean—what they call 'ghost winds'?" Bud asked breathlessly.

Tom nodded. "I only hope we can ride 'er out— no telling how long it'll last."

Tom knew that these windstorms in the ionosphere travel as fast as a thousand miles an hour. Unlike the ones that occur nearer the earth, the aerial tides flow for a certain time in one direction and then without warning reverse themselves.

This reversal was exactly what Tom wished might happen. The shift in current would free the rocket from the raging flow of air and permit the ship to continue on its original course. Before he had a chance to express this hope aloud, the *Star Spear* suddenly stopped its erratic behavior, and then swooped upward under enormous acceleration.

"She's straightened out!" Bud cried. "The tracking signals are coming through again from the island."

After Tom explained to Jones what had taken place, he said to Bud, "We were lucky the ghost wind changed direction so soon, but dodging them is a problem we'll have to solve before we start carrying passengers. We may have to set up a meteorological station here."

"The dummy rocket didn't register any such interference," Bud observed.

"These storms race wild through the lower ionosphere," Tom replied. "The dummy was just fortunate not to hit one."

"Do you think you can figure out a way to protect spaceships against them?" Bud asked.

"I believe it can be overcome by placing steering jets at different spots in the hull," Tom replied. "They'll go on automatically the moment the ghost wind hits the rocket ship."

"Wish we had a couple of those jets on here right now," Bud said. "Anyhow, we won't have to worry about the wind from now on. The air from here up will be so thin that the rocket won't even feel the storm when it hits."

Tom suddenly thought of the flight tape—it had probably been thrown out of line by the rocket's recent tumble in the ionosphere. A glance at the device confirmed his belief and Tom quickly made the adjustment, setting the tape in its proper position.

"Just in time," he murmured as a red light flashed and a buzzer sounded a warning that the first stage was about to detach itself.

"Check time!" came Jones' voice.

"Eighty-five seconds!" Tom responded. "First booster charge nearly ready to break off!"

The release clearance gun timer on the panel showed three—two—one!

The *Star Spear* quivered the moment the signal light went out, and explosions at the coupling points sent vibrations through the rocket ship.

"There it goes!" Tom cried. "Off clean as a knife cut!"

"And feel that release of pressure!" Bud whistled. "That neutralator really melts away the G's."

The massive sixty-motored base section dropped down and veered into its own separate line of flight, parachuting slowly back to earth. Radar control would keep the stage out of the paths of planes and ships before it plummeted into the ocean.

"Right on schedule," Tom announced. "We're seventy miles up."

"We're going faster every second," breathed Bud. "Time for a stretch."

Now that the booster had cut away, and they were pretty well out of the atmosphere and traveling at a constant acceleration, the boys knew it was safe to get up. Bud was first in releasing the catches of his take-off safety rack and sitting up. The hinged couch folded automatically and Bud climbed into his flight seat.

Tom followed him but continued to watch the various gauges and oscilloscopes as well as the flight tape. Sitting down next to Bud, he said:

"The next stage will drop off in sixty-three seconds." A moment later he commented, "Listen to those radio signals from the tracking platform! Jones has a perfect plot on us."

"Sure is a welcome sound," Bud added. "I don't feel so far from home. And speaking of home, how about taking a look?" When Tom nodded assent, Bud leaned over and began to remove the shutter from the starboard viewing port.

As the rocket rushed farther and farther from the earth, Tom reported to the field that the temperature and oxygen changes were being made perfectly.

"And the kicker in the second stage is working just as we planned," he concluded.

"You sure picked the right name for your invention!" Bud spoke up. "With that kicker hooked in, we've got about a million *mule*power!"

Tom smiled and glanced out of the porthole. The world was rapidly taking on its true spherical shape. Both land and ocean had a neutral gray-brown color, and the sky was no longer blue, but black.

"We're seventy-seven miles up," Tom announced into the radio, "and our speed is 5200 miles per hour."

There was no further communication from Fearing Island, and the boys wondered if the message had reached the instrument on the tracking platform.

A few minutes later the buzzer and warning light for the dropping of the next section interrupted the boys' discussion. The seconds ticked away and stage number two was successfully jettisoned. Number three cut in without a hitch.

The third stage would burn for fifty-nine seconds and cut out at an altitude of two hundred and seventy-eight miles. From this point the momentum of the *Star Spear* would carry them up with diminishing speed to the 1075-mile altitude stipulated by the contest.

At this altitude, in free flight, the race would begin! The rocket ship would circle the earth in exactly two hours.

The two boys looked at each other and grinned. Bud remarked, "No complaints on this trip. What say we skip the race and go right on to Mars?"

"Speaking of Mars," Tom said, "I'd better turn on the oscillograph. Our space friends might want to communicate with us."

"If it takes as long as usual to figure out their mathematical symbols," Bud said, "we'll be back home before you've deciphered the first sentence."

"That's where you're wrong, Bud."

From a compartment on the panel board Tom took out a notebook and opened it. On several pages were symbols with words beneath them. He explained that his father had been working night and day to compile this planet dictionary, as he called it. Mr. Swift had handed the booklet to his son just before the youth had entered the *Star Spear*.

"I had no idea it was so complete," Tom said, flipping the pages. "When Dad gets his teeth in a job, he sure doesn't let go until he's finished it."

Again the buzzer and warning light!

"Third stage is ready to go, Bud," Tom cried excitedly. "In a little while now we'll be in free flight!"

"And on our way to win a one-hundred-thousand-dollar prize," Bud added gleefully. "Tom, tell them we're going to take it up to Mars and convert it into Martian currency!"

The boys waited for the light to go out and the booster to drop off. Seconds went by. The light flickered off and on. Suddenly the blood drained from Tom's face as he noted that the flight tape was acting strangely. It was stopping and starting jerkily.

Without warning there came a series of terrific vibrations. It seemed as if the boys' stomachs would be torn out of their bodies. Their face muscles pulled down across their teeth. Their shoulders pained as though they had been struck by two down-swinging bats. A hot shudder raced through their bodies.

"The section must have jammed!" Tom cried, glancing at Bud.

But his friend had slumped forward, unconscious.

"Bud must have been caught off balance and clipped on the head," the young inventor thought. He knew that traveling at such high acceleration one's body and limbs feel heavy as lead, and muscle co-ordination is poor.

Tom reached for the automatic coupling clearance gun. Nothing happened!

"I've got to release that third stage before the motors quit firing!" he muttered frantically.

The young inventor knew that when the motors gave out he would no longer be able to steer, and the *Star Spear* would begin to tumble aimlessly, end over end. The nose section, if it could be launched at all, would be improperly aimed.

The motors were still firing—a tribute to the efficient performance of the kicker in conserving fuel. But he had to release the defective coupling before it was too late.

Gritting his teeth, Tom slid to the rear of the cabin, jumped into an overall heat-resistant work suit, and picked up a tool kit. After opening the hatch to the motor room, he descended to the heavy door of the stage below. Using an electronic lever, he waited impatiently while the door was opening.

The noise of the firing motors was deafening as he climbed along the magnesium girders to investigate the trouble. Each time the tail end swerved, Tom had to hang on for his life. He waited for the rocket to level momentarily, then crawled as fast as he could along the slender ribs of the section, hoping against hope that the fuel supply would not give out.

Finally, he reached the balky section containing the clearance guns. After the rocket had upended once more, Tom worked furiously to rip away the housing on the connection box. Then, resetting the controls so that the whole jettisoning operation could be worked manually, he put his hand into the box, and with one deft movement, spliced the necessary wires to close the connection.

He had to get back to the pilot's canopy before something else might go wrong. In this present position he could easily be spun off into space!

CHAPTER 21

AN UNEXPECTED MISHAP

AS THE *Star Spear* rushed upward, Tom heard one of the motors cough. The fuel supply in the third stage was coming to an end!

Doggedly he made his way back to the nose section. Suddenly the rocket began to swing sideways as a result of the uneven thrust of the motors. For a moment Tom hung suspended on the struts with his long legs dangling.

As the tail section reached the end of its swing and paused, before starting back the other way, the inventor climbed madly for a few seconds. Then he held fast while the section began another oscillation. This pattern of movement had to be repeated several times before Tom finally reached the opening at the center and pulled himself upward.

"I can thank my lucky stars for this!" he murmured, reaching the motor room of the payload stage.

Quickly he swung the lever to close the great hatch to the now almost useless section. Making sure it was absolutely tight, he hurried back to the pilot's canopy.

His friend was still slumped over, but Tom noted with relief that Bud seemed to be breathing regularly. Any attempt to revive him had to be deferred until the third stage was dropped.

A moment later the gyro showed the correct angle of flight. Tom pushed the manual control button for the release of the section and held his breath. Would it drop off?

Seconds later, the couplers were wrenched apart and the dead stage was jettisoned! The rocket ship shook crazily as it was freed from the dragging thirty-foot unit and the motors of the passenger stage cut in.

"Bud!" Tom cried, slapping his friend on the back. "Wake up!"

But Bud remained slumped over. A fearful thought took hold of Tom. Traveling at such fantastic velocity—nearly ten times as fast as sound—the effects of even relatively small bumps seemed enormously magnified and crushing to a flesh-and-blood body. Suppose Bud had been paralyzed by the sudden jolt he had received when the tail-assembly release mechanism had jammed!

Opening a compartment, Tom took out a vial of spirits of ammonia and held it near the unconscious boy's nose for a few seconds. His friend suddenly winced and his lips twitched.

When Bud's arm moved, Tom was sure that he would soon revive. Tom quickly returned to the pilot's seat to concentrate on the delicate job of guiding the *Star Spear* into orbital flight on the schedule set for it.

Against the loosening grip of the earth they had risen to a point almost one thousand miles high.

The motors in the nose section should now be swinging them out in a great arc toward the North Pole. A quick glance at the flight indicator was somewhat disturbing to Tom. They had been accelerating only slowly thus far, and according to his offhand recollection of their flight plan, they should have been a great deal farther northward than they found themselves.

Quieting his fears momentarily he turned his attention to Bud, who had just opened his eyes and was weakly trying to sit up.

"Where are we?" he asked groggily. "Are Sandy and Phyl okay?"

Tom smiled, relieved that his friend was going to be all right. "We're seven hundred miles away from our friends," he said, and told him about the knockout and the defective coupling. "Say," he cried suddenly, "here comes something on the oscilloscope!"

Bud, still half-conscious, was not interested. But Tom's eyes were focused on a mathematical symbol which was forming on the screen.

"A message from our space friends!" he exclaimed. Noting that the figure was different from the first one on the previous messages, he added, "I wonder if they're inviting us to meet them."

"Stop kidding," Bud murmured.

"There's a second figure!" Tom cried.

As he reached for the planet dictionary, Tom suddenly realized that it was extremely warm in the cabin. At first he thought that this was the natural result of their jets attaining such unprecedented speed. But by split seconds the pilot's canopy grew hotter and hotter.

"It's over 100 degrees in here!" Bud said. "Anything wrong?"

Tom looked at the cabin thermometer. It had climbed to 122 degrees and was still rising!

Pointing to a gauge, Tom cried, "The kicker isn't working! No wonder we haven't been accelerating properly."

"It's reading 850 now!" Bud exclaimed in alarm, knowing the gauge was expected to drop from a reading of 050 to 035 an instant after the fuel invention was put into operation. The fuel was streaming through the by-pass unchecked! It would be used up in two minutes, leaving none for the *Star Spear*'s return to earth!

Tom unstrapped himself and dived aft, telling Bud to get their space suits ready in case they should need them. Yanking open the rear wall panel, Tom saw, to his dismay, that the kicker and its feed lines were a mass of twisted, melted pipes. In spite of the fuel loss involved, Tom was grateful that the automatic valve had opened and diverted the fuel around the burned-out kicker. Otherwise, the fuel lines would have been plugged up, and an explosion would have resulted.

Tom pulled on a pair of asbestos gloves. With every moment a race against possible death, he tore out the damaged pipes with one hand and reached over with the other for the spare kicker which was clamped to the wall. Sweating and panting in the stifling heat, he inserted the new piping in a matter of seconds and lessened the opening through which the solar energy was being admitted. Then he called:

"Bud, what's happening on the gauge now?"

"It's going down—040—038—035. It's normal!"

Heaving a sigh of relief, Tom came back and once more strapped himself into the seat. He explained that evidently the excessive amount of solar radiation being admitted to the kicker had caused the over-heating.

By this time the cabin had become cooler; the thermometer read 90 degrees. Tom smiled in relief.

He checked the kicker gauge. It was still at the new figure and the speedometer told him that the rocket had accelerated even with the diminished fuel supply. Everything was working all right at the moment.

"If we can keep this up for just thirteen more seconds, we can stop worrying about the kicker," he said. "We'll be in free flight."

"We're doing 4300 miles an hour right now!" Bud cried. "And going faster every second. "What's our altitude?"

"Ten hundred miles," Tom replied, scarcely able to believe the reading.

The copilot whistled. "Wow! That was a speedy climb! Now for the race!"

At 1075 miles, Tom looked at Bud, then both stared at the orbital flight indicator. They were about to try the most daring thing man had yet attempted—to hurtle through space without the aid of human-made power.

When the indicator reached the null point, Tom threw over the ignition switch.

The kicker ceased to function. The motors died! There was an unreal silence!

CHAPTER 22

MESSAGES FROM SPACE

AFTER THE FIRST few seconds of orbital travel at 15,810 miles an hour, Bud remarked:

"Smoothest flight I ever had, Tom. And the easiest. Even this feeling of lightness in my hands and arms is rather pleasant, especially after that dropped-down feeling we had coming up. Say, this space-platform stuff wouldn't be so bad. I could almost live in an aerial houseboat and like it!"

"Sure you could, if it had a football field and a—"

Tom stopped speaking because new mathematical figures had started forming on the oscilloscope. The first signals had stopped when the overheating of the kicker had sent Tom scurrying to put in the new one. Now, the impulses were coming in fast and clear.

Once more, Tom grabbed the planet dictionary and began looking for the translation. His brow puckered. Finally he said:

183

"Bud, I believe this is a message from Dad. He can't contact us by radio, so he's trying this method."

"What does the message say?" Bud asked eagerly.

Tom admitted that he was puzzled. Evidently there were not enough symbols for Mr. Swift to send the message exactly. But after a few seconds of thought, Tom added grimly:

"I think the message is a warning that Rotzog took off and is determined to get us!"

"Good night!" Bud cried. "Do you think we can see him in time to avoid him at this speed, even with our radar?"

Tom groaned. "Rotzog's the most daring enemy I've ever had and probably the smartest. I only hope he hasn't perfected a radar signal good enough that he can pick *us* up!"

Bud had an inspiration. "You brought that super celestial telescope, didn't you? Let me look through it."

Tom took the telescope from a locker, handed it to his friend, and turned to use the transmitter to let his father know he had received the message. Just then a new set of dot-and-dash symbols began coming in. Tom studied the oscilloscope intently. Presently he reported to Bud, great excitement in his voice:

"Our race rival has launched his rocket in Australia ahead of time! Only a few minutes after we started!"

"Wow! The sky's getting jammed with rocketeers!" Bud commented. "Well, at least he's not planning to destroy us."

"No, but he *is* planning to win the race," Tom reminded his companion.

But Bud was confident of the *Star Spear*'s ability. "You have the race sewed up," he said with a grin.

"Here comes another message," Tom said.

As Bud scanned the sky with the telescope, Tom noted that the first two figures on the oscilloscope were the same as those in the original message that he and his father had received from their space friends. Now he was sure that this new set of mathematical symbols was from them instead of from the earth.

"Maybe they want to meet us out here," Bud suggested.

"No," said Tom, translating quickly. "They say we're running into trouble."

"Rotzog?"

"I don't think so."

The boys watched eagerly but no more figures appeared on the face of the oscilloscope. After a few seconds of waiting and watching, Tom looked up at the orbital flight indicator. Unnoticed, the indicator pointer had crept down from the zero position.

"Bud, look!" Tom said excitedly. "We're being swung off our course, out into space!"

A moment later their senses began to confirm the evidence of the sensitive instrument. They could feel the *Star Spear* pulling upward and to the right.

Startled by this unforeseen action, Tom weighed the possibility of using the rocket controls and returning the *Star Spear* to her course by a short burst of power from the rocket motors. Deciding on this course, he threw the ignition switch and instantly the motors roared to life.

After a few seconds his face became grave. "Bud, we've climbed another fifty miles off course!" he cried. "And I can't seem to fight the force that's sending us out of our orbit!"

He opened the throttle wider and the *Star Spear* reared. For a moment it seemed as if Tom had broken the hold of the mysterious force. But in another instant the ship yielded to the overpowering attraction and was gliding along its new and unknown line of flight.

"This must be the danger that message was trying to warn us against!" Bud exclaimed. "Could we be caught in the pull of another planet?"

"I doubt it," Tom replied. "We haven't traveled far enough from the earth to be influenced by another body."

"Then what can it be?" Bud asked. "Some trick of Rotzog's?"

"Perhaps."

Tom watched the panel for any meter indications that might give him a clue. He thought of the very great pull that "dead" stars can exert, but he knew that these bodies lay even farther out in space than the planets he had already considered.

His thinking was interrupted by the oscilloscope. Figures were appearing again.

"This may be the answer!" he said hopefully.

"Calling Swift!" the inventor translated.

It was a warning from the space beings that the

Star Spear was passing close to a meteor field. It had a magnetic attraction which was pulling the ship off its course and drawing it toward the whirling mass of destructive meteorites!

"We must get out of the field!" Bud exclaimed. "Can't we buck it?"

"Maybe we can," Tom replied, "but it'll use precious fuel."

"We must take the chance," Bud urged.

It seemed to Tom that their predicament resembled one of a helpless swimmer caught in a strong current. For the swimmer, the wisest course is not to buck the current, but to swim at a right angle to it until he has escaped its power.

The young inventor was jerked from his thoughts when another set of symbols appeared. "Race out of danger, at a right angle to your present course," they said. "Then we will send you directions to return to your orbital flight."

Elated at this confirmation of his own reasoning, Tom decided to obey. He turned the kicker to top capacity for five seconds, swinging sharp right, then cut off the motors.

Fervently hoping this had done the trick, he waited. The rocket seemed to stand still for a moment, then the magnetic pull began again, but this time it was not so strong.

"We're almost out of it!" Bud cried gleefully.

"One more maneuver. But we're farther from the earth," Tom said, worried, as he repeated the operation and found himself fifteen hundred miles high.

As promised by their benefactors, however, further instructions began to appear. Bud copied the symbols as Tom translated. He had just completed the preliminary directions, however, when the dots and dashes used to formulate the mathematical figures collapsed into a straight line and started to fade.

The boys watched intently, but the symbols no longer took shape. Then they died out completely.

Tom looked woefully at the figures he had copied. Without the rest of the instructions they were worthless.

"This is the finish," Bud said, his optimism gone.

Tom would not give up. He turned to the special transmitter he had brought and turned several small knobs.

"What are you going to do?" Bud asked.

"Try to reach those space people and get the rest of the directions," Tom replied. "If I ever needed to reach them, it's right now!"

Using the planet dictionary, he quickly copied a set of figures to read, "We need the instructions again."

He started transmitting. To attract their attention, he first sent the two initial figures that the mysterious friends had used in their messages to him. Then he added his own request. There was no reply.

"I'll try again," he told Bud. "If we don't raise them, we'll have to plot our own course."

Tom kept sending the symbols without a break for nearly a minute, but there was no response.

"Bud, give the motors another five-second burst

with the kicker on full. Let's get farther away from that magnetic field!"

The copilot complied and Tom continued to send. The maneuver completed, Bud asked:

"Any luck at all?"

"None," Tom replied, and transmitted the formula three more times but without success.

Then, suddenly, a flicker appeared on the oscilloscope!

Tom stopped sending and watched the scope. Another flicker followed the first. Dots and dashes appeared. A symbol formed. Then came figure after figure. The first three were the same as those Tom had translated before. Now a long string of figures was appearing.

"We have our answer!" Tom cried. "This is the escape route!"

CHAPTER 23

OMINOUS SIGNS

CLUTCHING HIS PAD, Bud copied the symbols quickly but carefully. Tom riffled through the pages as fast as he could, trying to keep up with the message while making a running oral translation.

The strange symbols stopped. With the course heading set, Tom burst into action.

"Give the kicker all she's got, Bud!" he called.

Bud pulled the kicker lever through its full arc.

Tom waited five ticks of the panel clock. "Now cut in the steering engines," he ordered.

Bud complied. Then Tom, following the space beings' complex navigational instructions, began to steer the *Star Spear* in a path around the edge of the powerful, invisible magnetic field.

According to the directions, in less than a minute the *Star Spear* was supposed to have escaped from the magnetic pull of the meteor field. Tom flipped off the switches of the steering motors and Bud pushed back the lever to cut off the kicker.

"Now we'll see," Tom said quietly.

Hardly daring to breathe, the anxious boys waited. For the next few moments there was a strange absence of any sensation in the rocket—practically no feeling of motion. Yet, according to the speedometer, they were still racing through outer space at well over eleven thousand miles per hour. It was not toward the meteors, however, but away from them.

"You did it, you old stargazer!" Bud exulted. "Whew! I don't want another scare like that one. I can tell you now that I sure was worried those signals were coming from Rotzog and would send us to our doom!"

Tom smiled. "I was myself for a while. But one of those figures set me straight. It's not a mathematical symbol which has ever been used on earth, so I figured Rotzog wouldn't know it."

"You mean the chicken's beak holding the worm? How is that translated?"

"I don't know. I had to skip it, Bud. Thank goodness it made no great difference." Glancing at the altimeter and the speedometer, he remarked, "In about eight minutes we should fall back into our orbital track."

Seven and a half minutes later the orbital flight indicator told Tom that the nose of the rocket was beginning to pull slightly to the right. The pull grew stronger and Tom once more briefly gunned the rocket ship motors to bring them back up to the 15,810-mile velocity necessary to keep the *Star Spear* in an orbital course.

Tom and Bud shook hands. They had escaped a slow death and words were futile to express their feelings.

Tom set up the cameras. As soon as the machines started working, Bud said, "These are going to be the miracle movies of our time. Especially the films we're taking on the revolving cameras. Those stars are going to show up wonderfully against that blackness of outer space. Say, where are we heading now, Tom?"

"We're on a diagonal course toward the Arctic Ocean," Tom replied.

"Pretty close to the abandoned Rotzog base," Bud remarked.

Fifteen minutes later the boys looked out and saw a marvelous spectacle. The morning sun gleaming down on the north-polar cap transformed the ice mass into a brilliant giant jewel of blinding beauty.

"What a place the poles would be to keep an operation secret from men in space!" Tom said. "With white equipment a project could never be observed!"

"Say," Bud spoke up, "where do you suppose Rotzog is? And our rival who took off from Australia?"

"I hope they're a thousand miles behind us and stay there!" Tom answered.

"If either of them show up, we'll have to depend on outmaneuvering them," Bud observed.

By this time the *Star Spear* was hurtling above the wastes of northern Siberia. Ahead, the glowing globe was darkening. By now the natives in the palm-thatched huts on the Philippines, Borneo, and Sumatra lay sleeping. Soon the boys were racing across the islands.

"What's our position now?" Bud asked, as he saw Tom turn on the space navigational instrument.

"We're 105 degrees east of Greenwich and 60 degrees south latitude," Tom replied, taking the reading. "Almost at the South Pole!"

The rocket soon passed over the Antarctic region and was heading for the lower shank of South America when morning began to break on this side of the earth.

Looking at the radarscope, Tom said, "Still no sign of Rotzog or our Australian rival!"

Tom continued to scan every direction with the radar screens. There was no trace of any rockets, meteors, or other interference.

"This is almost too easy," Bud complained, stretching his cramped muscles.

He had no sooner spoken than a pip on the radar indicated an object dead ahead, slightly above the course of their rocket.

"Rotzog!" Bud cried.

The image began to sweep at crazy angles, up, down, and across.

"It is no ordinary rocket!" Tom cried.

Instantly the idea flashed through his mind that this strangely maneuvering sky traveler must be the one belonging to the message senders.

"It's our space friends!"

"I hope so," Bud said. "I'd hate to be dropping in on an arsenal!"

On the scope the image of the dodging rocket grew larger as the *Star Spear* closed the distance between them.

"Tom!" Bud cried suddenly. "I just saw a couple of pips on the other radar tracker. It must be our Australian rival. For Pete's sake, don't hit one of those guys!"

Tom looked at the second scope and studied it for a couple of seconds. The image appeared again, faintly. He altered their course slightly to avoid a crash. Then he turned to the periscopic lens for a view of the area ahead.

"We'll be close enough to the mystery rocket to see it in a few seconds."

Suddenly the boys could see the outline of the mystery ship!

Tom signaled in the hope of attracting the attention of the other craft, but there was no response. Suddenly Bud called out:

"The image is still on the scope, but it's growing smaller."

"It's getting away!" Tom cried.

"But that's impossible," Bud retorted. "We're traveling at almost sixteen thousand miles an hour!"

"Now I'm sure that rocket contained our space friends!" Tom exclaimed. "I can understand that they might outfly us, but why would they turn tail and run?"

"Only one reason," Bud replied. "Rotzog *must* be around!"

CHAPTER 24

AN ATTACK

THE OUTLINE of the friendly spaceship disappeared completely from the radarscope, making the sixteen-thousand-miles-per-hour speed of Tom's rocket seem like a snail's pace by comparison.

"Say," said Bud, as a new idea struck him, "you don't suppose they thought this is Rotzog's ship? They're not equipped to defend themselves against an armed attack."

"It's possible," Tom replied. "Keep watching the scope, Bud," he directed. "If Rotzog is around, I want to know it."

Tom made a few calculations, then announced that they were about four minutes behind schedule, due to the delay in getting around the magnetic field.

"Well, can't we go faster and make up the time?" Bud inquired.

"We can go faster all right by turning on the

motors for a few seconds," Tom assured him. "But that won't solve our problem. If we go any faster, the earth can't hang on to us and we'll float up out of our orbit. Then we'll have that much farther to go."

Bud nodded comprehendingly and asked, "Well, what can we do?"

"The only thing I can figure out," Tom answered, "is to set the steering motors to fire in such a way that they will compensate for our increased centrifugal force and hold us down. I've just calculated what the settings ought to be. We'd better strap ourselves down. Everything that isn't fastened is literally going to hit the ceiling."

As soon as the boys were secured on their racks, Tom opened the kicker wide. The *Star Spear* accelerated and sustained the burst for ten seconds. Sliding his rack forward, Tom closed the arc and looked at the speed gauge.

Twenty-four thousand miles an hour!

When the pressure let up, Bud and Tom took their regular positions. Watching the screens intently as they swept the skies, the boys noted faint blips appearing on the radarscope.

"We sure made up the distance!" Bud gloated. "Man, that rival of ours won't have a chance against us now! We'll be back home collecting the prize before he gets out of orbital flight! That is," he added, "if Rotzog doesn't show up."

"He'll have to show up soon if he's still planning to," Tom said. "This race will be over for us in twenty-five minutes!"

Tom took a quick reading on his position finder. Far below, the sun was glinting on the Amazon River and to the west on snow-capped mountains.

"It's in the bag!" Bud chortled. "Tom, you can—"

His sentence was cut short by a tremendous flash of light through the porthole, followed by a faint, ominous vibration of the *Star Spear*.

"Tom, look at that scope!" Bud cried. "The screen's alive with pips!"

"They're guided missiles!" Tom groaned. "Rotzog has found us!"

"For Pete's sake, let's get out of his path!" Bud urged.

Tom knew that the only way to do this was to change his course. And to change his course at this point in the race was the last thing he wanted to do.

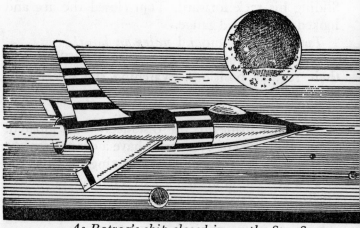

As Rotzog's ship closed in on the Star Spear,

With victory so close, the inventor hated the thought of consuming valuable seconds trying to evade Rotzog. At best, their lead over the Australians was tenuous; the difference between victory and second place might be a matter of seconds.

"But I can't be blasted out of the sky, either," Tom told himself.

He decided to use a maneuver that would not consume much time and might throw his enemy off. Quickly he reached over to the controls and shut off the steering rockets. The ship was still traveling at a faster than orbital speed, and the *Star Spear* instantly responded by rising sharply to let a barrage of missiles pass harmlessly below. Seconds later, Tom cut in the steering motors to push the ship earthward.

Alternately firing and stalling the rockets, Tom was able to make the *Star Spear* describe an erratic, undulating path that made it impossible for Rotzog

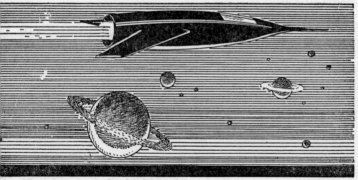

Tom opened the kicker wide

to fire on him accurately. The missiles launched at them were unable to follow the roller-coaster course Tom set for them and either missed by wide margins or blew up harmlessly ahead or astern.

Bud's face was lined with worry. "Tom, these maneuvers will use up all our fuel. There'll be none left to take us back to earth!"

"I think that's exactly Rotzog's idea," Tom replied grimly. "If he can worry us enough, the fiend can count on stranding us out in space."

"Here he comes in person!" Bud announced.

Tom looked at his fuel gauges. He could not do much more dodging.

The enemy rocket, roaring from the right rear, was now in position to make a direct pass at Tom's ship. The *Star Spear* stood completely exposed to a broadside attack! If he tried to swing away, Rotzog would be right on his tail. Tom knew he must gamble on using another tremendous amount of fuel to avert this attack.

As Rotzog's ship closed in at point-blank range, Tom opened the kicker wide, dived, and rolled under the oncoming enemy ship!

CHAPTER 25

A RECORD VICTORY

TRAVELING for a few seconds at thirty thousand miles per hour, Tom and Bud stared in fascination at the speedometer. For a moment thoughts of Rotzog were erased from their minds. But the next moment, the boys realized that the terrific speed was fast-consuming their fuel supply and straining every part of the *Star Spear*.

Tom, after swooping under Rotzog's rocket, had swerved in a parallel line to his orbital flight. Sure that Rotzog could not overtake him now, he rose in a diagonal course until he met the orbit, then turned off his fuel. Tom knew he had used more than was advisable.

Bud had not taken his eyes from the radarscopes, but no further pips had appeared. This time, Tom had outmaneuvered his enemy!

"Where are we?" Bud asked.

"Over the Isthmus of Panama." For a minute

Tom forgot the gravity of the situation and smiled. "First stop San Francisco!"

"I hope my mother and dad will be there to meet us," Bud wished aloud. "It sure will be good to see them."

"My folks and the Newtons will barely have time to make it in the *Sky Queen*," Tom commented.

"Say, I hadn't thought of that," Bud reflected. "Imagine! We will have gone all around the world in the same time it takes them to get from Fearing Island to San Francisco."

Tom smiled. "It sort of proves the truth of the old saying about the longest way round being the shortest way home. What time is it, anyway?"

"One forty-five."

There was a sudden crackling on the radio. It had been silent for so long that the boys were startled to hear it.

"International Code," Tom said. "An S O S, Bud, from Rotzog! His motors won't fire and he's almost out of fuel!"

There was a silence of several seconds, then a request for an answer.

"Don't give him one. It's a trap!" Bud declared.

Tom was in a quandary. As Bud had suggested, an answer to Rotzog might give him a fix on their position and permit one last attack. On the other hand, he could not ignore a genuine plea for help.

A repetition of the message from Rotzog decided Tom. "Let's risk it," he said to Bud, and began to tap out an answer.

"This is Tom Swift. What happened? Where are you?" Tom repeated the message.

After a short pause came an answer. "Rotzog speaking. Johnson is with me. We're drifting into space. Our air conditioner's going bad. We'll roast to death! You must help us!"

"You must help them!" Bud exclaimed heatedly. "Five minutes ago they were shooting at us! Now, Rotzog has the nerve to ask you to save them!"

Tom was already sending out a message requesting more information about their fuel.

"We're using oxygen-alcohol mixture. Johnson gave me a description of your secret apparatus and I built an ozone converter like yours. On our last pass at you, it failed. Have only two thousand gallons of fuel left."

"What's your position?" Tom asked. "And the composition of your fuel?"

Bud gazed at Tom incredulously. "You aren't really planning to help those guys, are you?" he asked in disbelief.

"I don't really know whether we can yet," Tom answered, "but I'm beginning to get some ideas. Let's feed his radio signals into the Spacelane Brain and find out what his position and course are. We can learn whether that much of his story is true, anyway."

Tom listened intently as Rotzog answered, then said to Bud, "He's using one of the first mixtures I tried. It became inactive at fast rates of flow. It can be reactivated."

The Spacelane Brain confirmed Rotzog's position and verified that he was not far behind Tom in the same orbital track.

"Rotzog and Johnson really are in bad shape," Tom said. "I can't stand by and see them roast from solar radiation."

"Guess you're right," Bud agreed.

Tom tapped, "Rotzog, have you any silver nitrate with you?"

Rotzog gave an affirmative reply and Tom quickly gave instructions. "Uncover your ozone converter and slowly pour through the catalyst bed a solution of silver nitrate. This will rejuvenate the invention you borrowed from me. On your way down, restrict the flow of fuel through it. Don't open your throttle wide."

This time, Rotzog did not reply and Bud snorted. "He didn't even thank you. Say, Tom, aren't you going to capture him when he comes down?"

"You bet I am," Tom said grimly. Then, looking at his watch, he said, "We'd better forget him now and worry about our own landing. Our rocket ship's over Lower California, and we must decelerate.

"Turn on that flight tape recorder, Bud," he requested.

As Bud did so, the two boys looked at each other in pleased satisfaction. The race was almost over!

Suddenly Tom's elation turned to concern as he glanced at the fuel gauges. In order not to crash, he had to get every degree of energy possible from solar radiation.

Tom began to decelerate and kept this up until at two hundred miles above the earth the *Star Spear* was nearly down to zero velocity. To his relief, the kicker was still working!

Bud, seeing the pleased expression on his friend's face, reached over and said, "Inventor boy, you've even fooled yourself!"

"Yes, I have," Tom admitted quietly.

At sixty miles up the kicker stopped working and Tom cut in the regular fuel line. But the worry about conserving the fuel was over.

The flight tape recorder nicely engineered the difficult descent through the outer layer of air. The *Star Spear* was reversed, so that the thrust of the motors was upward to brake their descent.

Within a few minutes the boys could distinguish the outline of San Francisco and soon they were hovering five thousand feet over the Navy airport.

"Look at the crowd!" Bud cried, as they drew near the field.

Excited people were rushing about, cars were arriving in droves. News cameras were mounted on building tops. Television equipment stood poised on the runway.

"There's the *Sky Queen!*" Tom cried. "My folks are here!"

After receiving clearance to land, Tom slowly throttled down the motors, and amidst the cheers of the crowd, set the history-making craft down on its magnesium cylinder landing legs on the runway in front of the administration building.

The space-defeating rocket swayed slightly as the landing-weight distributor moved a fraction to bring the craft level. Tom turned off the engines and beckoned Bud to crank open the heavy, airtight door.

As the two boys looked out, the applause became tremendous. They waved and gave an overhead handclasp. Waving back at them frantically were the Swifts, the Newtons, and the Barclays.

Tom suddenly noticed the large airport clock. It showed the time to be only 9:20.

"Look a that clock, Bud!" he laughed. "We left Fearing Island at ten. We've traveled around the world in minus forty minutes!"

"It's a good thing this isn't Singapore." Bud grinned. "Or we'd be getting there yesterday!"

By this time the newsmen, photographers, and telecasters were milling around the *Star Spear*. The boys posed and made statements.

Eyes popped when Tom told his audience of his encounter with Rotzog and Johnson, and said the authorities should be notified to pick them up. A policeman hurried off to do this, while a reporter told the boys that Radnor, led by a fisherman, had found Rotzog's hide-out in the Aleutians. Though the rocket ship had been launched by the time they reached it, all Rotzog's workers had been captured.

"And now, Tom Swift," the reporter said, "before you go, tell us what your next invention will be."

Tom laughingly shrugged, not knowing at the moment that it would be his *Giant Robot*.

Tom asked if there was news yet of the rocket that had taken off from Australia.

"Not yet," a TV man replied.

At last the boys' families and friends were able to push their way through the crowd.

"It just doesn't seem possible, Tom!" Mrs. Swift said, hugging her son affectionately. "Congratulations, my dear."

"Thank you, Mother."

Sandy threw her arms around her brother and said, "Next trip I want to be your copilot. How about it?"

"And take my job away from me?" Bud called. "Never!"

"But we might make it a foursome," Tom said, smiling at Phyl Newton. She stood on her tiptoes and blushingly kissed him.

"Any souvenirs of the trip?" Mr. Swift asked, after a firm handshake with his son and a slap on the back.

"You're the only person we brought a gift to," Tom replied. "Your dust collector is full of mineral particles from space—every color of the rainbow."

At this moment Mr. Hopkins and two other members of the Rocket Commission walked up to claim their sealed instruments. Though much of the data enclosed would not be made public for some time, Mr. Hopkins confirmed that the *Star Spear* had indeed made an orbital flight around the earth.

As the commissioners congratulated the boys, a reporter came running to the group with a double news flash. Rotzog had been apprehended in Lower California. And secondly, the rival rocket had been unable to finish the race because of a fuel shortage. It had landed on a small island off Bermuda.

"Too bad," Tom remarked, but his friends did not agree.

Mr. Hopkins stepped forward. Clasping Tom's hand, he said over a microphone:

"That means you win the race! . . . The prize of one hundred thousand dollars, and the honor that goes with it, is awarded to eighteen-year-old Tom Swift!"